# The Evil Locked Within

P. J. Mayhair

*The Evil Locked Within*
*Copyright © 2016 P. J. Mayhair*
*All rights reserved.*

## Also by P. J. Mayhair

**Novel:**

The Evil Locked Within

**Short Stories:**

"One Last Play" in Opus 22 by Melius Scripto Press International.

**Coming soon:**

Her Last Nights and Other Tales of Terror

*This book is dedicated to my wife Maggie and my son Oliver.*

# CHAPTER ONE

Jeremiah enjoyed the miniature steam-filled screams escaping the mixture of eggs in the pan. The sizzling smell tickled his nose and his mouth watered. He was so hungry from work that afternoon that he had to cook himself a little evening snack. He fluffed the eggs in the pan with a fork and added a bit of salsa. The spiciness was a pleasure he wasn't allowed to indulge in. Spice was considered sinful.

He reached to the side of the cabinet and turned up the volume on the television as the news report came back on.

"Another update in the case of the Hayfield Serial Killer murders this evening."

Jeremiah held the pan just under his mouth and forked the hot, gooey snack into it. He knew Mother would not have approved, but he didn't have time to sit and eat properly. He didn't want to keep her waiting.

"Fingerprints have been found on the third victim: Caroline Nutt. They were found hidden on the inside of her arm," the news anchor announced.

Jeremiah's ears perked up; his fork hanging in the air, a piece of egg quivering.

"Per Detective Leroy Banks, the prints have come back to a Mr. Samuel Hall. Mr. Hall was the boyfriend of the deceased and has been taken in for questioning. Neighbors report hearing Miss. Nutt and Mr. Hall arguing recently."

A photo of Caroline Nutt and Samuel Hall appeared on the screen. They seemed to be on a beach somewhere. The two twenty-somethings looked terribly upset with each other.

Jeremiah laughed a little; spraying eggs and salsa onto his chin. He wiped his mouth and turned off the television set. He continued to eat his eggs; enjoying the burning sensation on his lips from the burnt little peppers.

When he finished, he sat the pan in the sink and went back into the living room. His bag was waiting for him in the doorway that separated the two rooms.

The fading portrait of his Mother looked down at him. Her gaze was judgmental and stern, but he loved her just the same. That was the last portrait she had painted of her. Grandfather had thought that cameras were the tools of the Devil and hippies – *and don't get me started on those computers* – so he insisted portraits be painted instead. He had commissioned the one in the living room not too long before he died. His Grandfather didn't even live to see it finished.

Grandfather hadn't been sick, as far as Jeremiah could remember. He just passed in his sleep one night. His house, and the life he had worked so hard for, passed onto Jeremiah's mother. She had smiled when she found out the house would be in her name. The smile was not kind or warm and it stuck with him forever. But, they would be well off for the foreseeable future.

Unfortunately, for the painter, her happiness wasn't until after her sitting. The last portrait of her was locked in that unforgiving snarl. Her eyes were downcast, and from where the painting was placed on the wall, she could look down and judge her baby boy for the rest of his life.

"I'm sorry, Mother. I left that dish dirty in the sink."

*Filth!*

"Please don't, Mother!"

Flinching, he threw up a hand to his face. He felt the painting reach out to get him, but he turned his back to her, hoping she wouldn't catch him. Running to the kitchen, he went straight to the sink and turned the hot water on without bothering the cold faucet. A cloud of steam surrounded him. He dropped the bag and grabbed the mangled pad of steel wool wedged on the side of the faucet. It still had some soap caked on it, so he dug into the pan.

The cast iron surface was clean without much effort but he continued to scrub, regardless. He moved from the pan to the handle, scrubbing and scouring. The steel wool was losing pieces of itself as it assaulted the old iron skillet. He rinsed the pan under the near boiling water and placed it in the drying rack.

The filth left on his hands was horrific. Little flecks of iron and steel mixed with egg and salsa, clung to the creases in his palm.

The steel wool made long deep circles on his pale skin. He dug in between his fingers, then ground the steel wool into his nailbeds. Red welts plumped up under his skin in the boiling water. His hands trembled as the skin threatened to open and spill blood into the stainless-steel basin.

He dropped the steel wool in the sink. Careful to use the back of his hand, he turned off the water, unwilling to risk the chance of dirtying his fingers again. He walked back into the living room, holding the large duffle bag in his hands. Bowing his head under the portrait of his mother, he let the duffle bag fall to his feet. Taking a somber breath, he crossed himself.

"In the name of the Father, the Son, and the Holy Ghost…"

He prayed to the portrait; he prayed for her forgiveness.

The pain of her stare subsided when he finished. He picked up the duffle bag by the thick strap, shouldering it with a little extra effort. The solid lump shifted as he moved the strap. He pushed it back into a more manageable shape on his hip.

"She was *too* much."

He walked out the door and locked it securely behind him. There were three deadbolts, with three different keys, he could never be too careful. The street was quiet except for the tiny crunch of his boots grinding on the road, encumbered by his heavy load. Normally, he would take his truck and his shoulder, weighted down with his duffle bag, would have agreed. Not tonight though, tonight he was throwing caution to the wind. The church wasn't that far away from his house. Besides, he needed the exercise.

The setting sun warmed his back as he walked down Third Street. When he got to the intersection of Third and South West Dallas Street, he found his destination. The First Presbyterian Church stood solemn, full of history and hell, looming against the heavy purple sky.

The building was only one-story, a humble church for a busy town. There weren't many Presbyterians in Hayfield, but the church was still full on Sundays. The parking lot only held a few dozen cars in the morning, so many of the patrons had to park on the grass or on the other side of the road. He couldn't imagine the people living in the houses appreciated that.

There was only one car in the parking lot tonight. It must belong to the pastor, working late. The light from the pastor's study on the far side of the church glowed with fake warmth, near the back of the building.

Jeremiah turned around, observing the other side of the street, checking if any of the small brick houses were producing snooping neighbors There was still a little bit of light outside. There were still some orange lights glowing in some homes but all the blinds and curtains were pulled shut. It was risky doing this in the early evening when he could have waited, hidden by the night. But right now, the street was unaware of his existence. He turned back to his goal.

In Jeremiah's opinion, The New Presbyterian Church was quite lovely. It had one small Catherine window facing the street that was about three feet tall. The basic rose shape that the panes created was pretty in its simplicity. They were not filled with colored glass or any gold leafing like the Catholic Church in town. They were plain frosted glass, appearing diamond encrusted to any passersby on the street during the day. Jeremiah understood why Megan, his date earlier, was a member here.

He set down the black duffel bag. Opening the side zipper, he pulled out one of his thick latex gloves, he had heard that the thinner gloves still could leave fingerprints. Although he wasn't sure if that was true, he didn't want to risk it. Taking a step back, he fully unzipped the bag and tried to decide on how he wanted to arrange her.

He pulled Megan's head out of the bag and placed it upright under the window. Her face was pale from hanging in the Letting Room for so long. But her lips were still red and her eyes were just as green as they had been when he first saw her. He loved her eyes.

"I should have kept them."

But it was too late for that.

When they first met, she had mentioned she was Presbyterian so he wanted to be as respectful as possible. He brought her here without knowing if this was the right church or if she even went to church, for that matter. It was the thought that counted, anyway.

"Ha. Just like Christmas," he mumbled.

Adjusting her lovingly and carefully, he could balance her head without it falling over. He brushed a few strands of her shoulder-length brown hair away from her face. The red tips of her hair had curled up and gotten stuck in the crusted mess where her lips had been.

He pulled her arms and legs out of the bag. They were still a bit heavy, despite being drained. Megan had been a rather full figured girl. He had not been with a woman before, but something stirred inside him. It had driven him to ask her out. He was almost shocked when she agreed.

He arranged the rest of her appendages in the shape of a star, right below her head. He frowned.

"Darn it."

He only had four sides and needed a fifth to make the one horizontal line to finish the shape. There was nothing he could do now; he would have to let it go. It would still have the desired effect.

He loved it. The cops, the silly media, everybody, would try to make some insightful leap as to what the star meant. There wasn't any real meaning to it, though.

*Well, maybe.*

He had gotten the inspiration from Megan. She had a small star-shaped birthmark on her right breast. Since he had kept her breasts in a large coffee can in his fridge; he decided to leave her with a star of a different sort.

A slight giggle escaped him at his next idea. To thoroughly confuse everyone, he placed her body in the middle of the star, rotated upside down, away from the head. Again, no real reason other than to mess with Detective Banks' head on the news. No doubt it would keep them wondering.

He wished to kiss her one last time, he loved this one. He loved them all, no matter how dirty Mother said they were. The urge to bend down was strong, but he fought it off. She may have condemned all of science to demonic teachings, but Jeremiah still understood the concept of DNA. There was enough explanation on the news about how it had caught people.

Shouldering the nearly weightless bag, he walked back towards home. This one was close by, which made him happy. He hated having to drive far out to remote locations. Especially places he was not too familiar with. Even though he lived in Hayfield his entire life, there were still parts he hadn't fully explored. He had other things to do.

The bag swung lazily in rhythm with his body and he wondered if he would have time for dinner when he got home. Those eggs were getting lonely in his stomach. There was a new recipe he wanted to try with the ingredients in the coffee can in the fridge.

# CHAPTER TWO

As he drove through the cycloptic green light, he watched his prey go by him mindlessly. Most people in town didn't notice Jeremiah, despite him being a long time local. But he liked it that way. To be honest, being noticed was detrimental to his... *lifestyle*. He laughed at his own choice of words; continuing his drive down the street to the market.

Mr. Lipmann's Market had been in Hayfield forever, it seemed. His grandfather talked about going there when he was a kid. Just like Jeremiah, he was always being sent there to pick up groceries for his mother. The real Mr. Lipmann was long dead, but the new owner was Gabriel Lipmann. The wiry old man was always nice to him.

Gabriel had been friends with his mother. He

gathered that much from their brief talks. Mother had never mentioned being friends with Gabriel, she barely acknowledged that the man even worked there. However, when Gabriel talked about her, his eyes would glaze over and he would get starry-eyed. Jeremiah liked to think she had at least one admirer.

That's why he went to Mr. Lipmann's, instead of the grocery chain a few blocks down. While other "regular" people went to work; Jeremiah went to the grocery store.

Doing so in the middle of the day had its own advantages. It kept him out of the public eye and he was able to live without working. He had never had to work, not even a summer job. His mother didn't need to work either. She was always home to watch him; doing everything she could for Jeremiah.

His grandfather had owned the local bank in town for years until one of those national banks came into town and bought it from him. They had paid him nicely enough to take care of his family for multiple generations.

Gabriel's smiling face greeted him as he walked into the store. His olive skin had started to grow a little dull, matching the snow that had started falling on his head. Despite his age, his eyes were still sharp, and his mind was even sharper. He still rang up customers without using the till. He calculated the taxes and discounts in his head. It was an admirable talent, one that Jeremiah wished he had.

"Good morning, Jerry," Gabriel said.

"Good morning, Mr. Gabriel," he answered cheerfully.

Jeremiah smiled at the nickname "Jerry." Mother called him that when he was being a good boy. Since Gabriel was a friend of hers, Jeremiah appreciated the small connection to her.

"What are we looking for today?" Gabriel asked as he leaned against the counter.

He did that often, more now than in past years, as he was suffering from a degenerating hip. Working at that store, stocking boxes, wrestling with the occasional drunk on Saturday nights, and standing beside a register for hours on end had not been kind to his joints.

Jeremiah didn't like the idea that Gabriel wouldn't be around very much longer. In a way, he had grown to care for the man, and in the end, it would be alright. Gabriel would finally be reunited with Jeremiah's Mother.

"I'm just looking for more bleach," Jeremiah said.

He knew the store as well as Gabriel as he strolled

down the correct aisle. He grabbed a gallon of the off-brand bleach and, for good measure, a second box of steel wool. Briefly, he thought about buying a bag of candy but dismissed the idea. His mother would not approve of him ruining his teeth with sugar. When he got to the counter, Gabriel was laughing.

"You sure go through a lot of this stuff, ya know? Your mom was just as much of a cleaner. Nothing was ever clean enough for her." He shook his head, lost in some far-gone memory of Jeremiah's mother.

Gabriel bagged the bleach and steel wool. Jeremiah left without making any more small-talk. Gabriel had already checked out of their conversation, lost in memories of long ago. Sometimes talking about his mother was hard for Jeremiah, he didn't feel like it today. Murmuring a goodbye that Gabriel probably didn't hear, he walked back to his truck. He had plenty of cleaning to do back home.

# CHAPTER THREE

The tangy smell of chlorine gas soothed his nerves. The blood on the table had turned almost black now that it was dry. Jeremiah scrubbed in soft, slow circles so as not to risk scratching the table. As he worked, his lips watered at the copper smell.

He hadn't started cleaning at first. When he had gotten home he stripped, folding his clothes, and set them on the kitchen counter. When he went downstairs, he laid down, relaxing in what was left of Megan. This time, his date had left him a treat: she had soiled herself in the first spasms of fear.

The table cleaned up easily, especially in comparison to his inherited large oak table. He had used the wooden table at first, but it soaked up everything, becoming much too dirty to clean. So, using his inheritance, he replaced the wooden table with a stainless-steel autopsy table. He had gotten it at an auction along with some handy little medical devices. It was quite lucky that the college sold off their old pieces to collectors when they got new ones.

He didn't get rid of the wood table; though. His Mother would've been too disappointed. Instead, he repurposed it into a shop table for some of his heavier equipment.

He left the main room, going through the door that led to the Letting Room. In here, he washed the handcuffs that were suspended from the ceiling. There were bits that had stuck to them. Once clean, he worked some oil into the hinges to keep them from freezing up. The ones on the floor were still clean. She hadn't needed those.

*Her legs were plenty spread, Jerry. You could have caught something.*

"Mother, please."

Jeremiah shook the images out of his mind. She was right, though, as always. Megan was performing acts on a man behind a club the night before their date. Despite her mannequin-like beauty, Jeremiah still had to wash her; twice, with bleach and steel wool. He didn't want to dirty himself when playing with her.

Eventually, the basement was clean enough for his mother's expectations. The bleach had washed the blood away from the walls and tools, and they swirled together in the drain on the concrete floor in a soup of cleaning liquids and body fluids. The drain entered directly into his new septic tank so that the city would not know what a mess his house made.

His skin began to tingle; he was still dirty from where he had laid on the table. The brown crusty mess was starting to crack on his skin. He left the basement and went up the steps and through the kitchen. In the living room, he tried his best to dodge under the gaze from the portrait. He didn't want her to see him in his current state. He knew she would not approve, and he knew how she would want him to clean.

*You are filthy!* She had caught him.

"Yes, Mother. I'm going upstairs to clean myself now."

*See that you do. And do not get any on the upholstery.*

Jeremiah hung his head. Upstairs, inside his bathroom he turned the hot water on until steam filled the air, making the gold flaked, white tiles slick. He stepped under the water, causing the dried blood and feces to reactivate on his skin. It dripped down his body and swirled around his feet into the drain.

He grabbed the steel wool off the soap dish, running it up and down his arms. Softly at first, the scrubbing increased in intensity to make sure that he got any trace of body fluids off the fawn-colored hair on his skin. He took the scrubber to his face, scouring the steel across his lips, scrubbing away the memory of her kiss. He scrubbed down to the hair on his chest and thought of how good Megan had felt the night before.

In an instant, the memories affected him. A tingle had worked its way from the primal center of his brain, down his spine, and into his groin. He looked down between his legs and saw what those dirty thoughts did to him. He wept.

"I'm sorry, Mother."

*So disgusting. Put it away or I'll cut it off.*

He sniffed back the rest of his tears. "Please, don't cut it off. I'll clean it."

Taking his shameful reminder of masculine filth into his hands, he pulled his foreskin back and scrubbed the head in short, jagged stabs. He had to make sure to get all the crevices where traces of Megan could hide. The pain was his punishment, just as he had been told as a child.

Once he was sure it was clean and sanitary again, he turned off the water. He rubbed himself down with the towel but decided against the robe. He laid on his bed, enjoying the soft sheets on his naked skin.

Thoughts of where he would hunt next drifted in and out of his mind. The impending thrill threatened to dirty him again. He pushed the feeling aside for later and nodded off to sleep.

# CHAPTER FOUR

Jeremiah's truck rolled down the road, choking and sputtering. The dirty fuel injectors had become so corroded that there was no cleaning them anymore. He would have to get them replaced... eventually. He didn't have the time for that, and he really didn't want to spend the money.

The money his grandfather had left them would have bought a brand-new truck, years before, at least. Instead, he had spent nearly all the family fortune on his house. While his unsuspecting neighbors upgraded and modernized their homes, Jeremiah had the walls double insulated. The windows were replaced with thicker double panes so that sounds could barely be heard. It was the best investment he could have made.

In his truck, his fingers tapped on the steering wheel as he whistled along with the hymnal on the radio. The AM station always kept his spirits up. He would have liked to have gone to church on Sundays, but Mother had always said that the church was full of false worshippers. She promised that if he went there, his soul would be taken into the eternal darkness and damnation. He didn't want that. He would remain a good man, for Mother.

He came to a stop at the red light and watched the people walk across the street. It would have been easy to just depress the gas pedal. But, no, he was a good man. He didn't like causing pain. He wondered if people knew how close they came to death every day of their lives. *Can you feel me in control?*

He smiled through the glass at a small platinum-haired girl as she skipped through the intersection. She was holding onto an elderly lady that he assumed was her grandmother. A large, golden ponytail bounced up and down in rhythm with her movement. She stopped skipping when she noticed Jeremiah smiling from inside his truck. She waved, and he waved back over his steering wheel.

Her grandmother, startled by the sudden lack of movement, glanced over to see what she was doing. Her eyes locked on to Jeremiah and he smiled kindly. She pulled the little girl closer into the folds of her dress as she scolded her. There was no doubt in Jeremiah's mind that the girl was being told some cautionary tale about strangers or something similar.

*No, sweetie, you're too young. You haven't been tainted by evil. Even Mother wouldn't think so.*

At that moment, he was a boy of only six. He stood naked in the kitchen, trying not to rub the pulsating burn across the back of his legs. The wooden spoon had cracked down the center on the third pass across his skin. Mercifully, they didn't have a spare so his punishment had been cut short. He knew that he deserved it, though. He had been caught talking to the neighbor girl outside.

Her name was Chelsea. Jeremiah loved to say her name all the time. She was thirteen, over twice his age, and her face was more beautiful than her name. She had been walking down the sidewalk, heading back to her house from town. He had been sent out to check the mail for Mother and he lingered until she walked by him. He had expected her to keep walking, ignoring him. Instead, she stopped.

"You look like you just walked out of one of those ol' black and white movies!"

She had giggled. His face had turned red, burning with blood under the skin. At the time, he didn't fully understand that he was dressed differently than the other boys his age.

Even in 1977, when everyone's clothes were full of color and their thoughts were filled with colorful ideas, he was dressed in a black vest and small black leather shoes. His suspenders kept up his tight grey trousers, and he always had on a bow tie, blue on this occasion. His mother had a classic taste, and she dressed him accordingly.

Chelsea understood how she embarrassed him. Red-faced, she offered an apology.

"I'm sorry. I wasn't trying to make fun of you." Her eyes fell to her hands as her voice became softer. "You actually look quite handsome." She looked back up with a sweet little smile crossing her lips. Jeremiah's face reddened further, but for a different reason.

"Thank you." He found himself staring at her bright dress. "You're very colorful."

She smiled, but it erupted into a melodic giggle. She put her arms out, twirling in a circle like a ballerina. The flashes of color coming off her cotton summer dress reminded him of a kaleidoscope. He stared slack-jawed at the dazzling sight in front of him. It was too bad for both of them that his mother was also watching.

She came barreling down the driveway from the house, screaming at the top of her lungs. Her face was beet red, and the veins in her neck crawled up her cheeks, trying to escape. In one hand, she clenched a dish rag; in the other hand was a long wooden spoon she had been using to boil cabbage.

Jeremiah understood what was about to happen. It was all too common for Mother to act this way. She called them her "fits of repentance," even though she acted as if she didn't remember what she had done during these fits. It was all quite confusing.

Chelsea didn't know what was happening, and Jeremiah wished every day from then on that he had warned her. Chelsea just stood there, her dress still flowing slightly from the momentum of the twirl. Her mouth was just barely opened, staring in disbelief at the rampaging woman headed straight for her.

Before she could move, the towel flew through the air like bolas. It wrapped itself around the girl's slender waist. When the dish towel flew close over Jeremiah's head he had smelled the chlorine. Chelsea smelled it too, once it wrapped itself around her middle. The terrible realization of what would happen to her dress spread across her face.

"Clean off those disgraceful markings, you trollop," his mother screamed. She brandished the spoon that had tasted his backside many times before.

Chelsea's face twisted. It was the face of someone that wanted to yell, to rage. Instead, water poured down her cheeks. She turned and ran down the street. Jeremiah would never see her again.

Jeremiah could just barely hear her cry for her own mother. He knew better than to watch closely as she ran away. She had left him there; any more staring would earn him more lashings.

He turned to face his mother's wrath, but it didn't come. She let her hands fall down to her sides, breathing deeply. There would be no punishments outside. Outside was where the public could judge. His punishments always came, but they came in private.

She did not want the embarrassment of having to switch him outside. She wasn't worried about the neighbors' critique of her; she was looking out for how they thought of her boy. He loved how she always thought about his best interest.

She grabbed his hand with her free one. The smell of bleach overpowered him as he tried to keep up with her. For a large woman, she was quick; at least while he was still young.

Back in the kitchen, after his punishment, he was allowed to pull his britches back up. He hung his head shamefully while she once again scolded him on the evils of girls and women.

"They are no good for you, son. Any girl that has had the monthly Devil is only there to use her feminine parts to drag you into the fiery pits of Hell."

She paced back and forth in the kitchen, her eyes darted frantically like she was seeing the demons coming. She was trying, with all her soul, to keep them away. He was happy that she wouldn't look at him. Her angry eyes were always different. They were cold, full of spite, and almost black.

A screaming horn blared from behind him, making him jump and he was back at the stop light. It had turned green, and he hadn't even noticed. The shiny silver Mercedes behind him *had* noticed and decided it was its civic duty to inform him of the change.

As Jeremiah began to drive through the intersection,

he checked his rearview mirror. He wanted to see if the driver of the Mercedes was a possible new date. Much to his dismay, it was an elderly man, maybe in his sixties. Jeremiah threw a wave into his mirror to apologize and took a left at the next light.

# CHAPTER FIVE

Jeremiah hadn't found the perfect woman yet, but he needed to pee. He was on East Main Street where all the car dealerships had been built to showcase their shiny little toys, for people trying to drive through Hayfield as fast as possible. That is if they just didn't use Interstate 30 and completely bypass his town.

The traffic brought many lovely ladies for him to choose from. He especially loved watching the younger women pick out sports cars. The euphemism of them driving a large red convertible made him snicker, while he decided what their worth was. Next to one of the used car dealerships was a gas station he particularly liked.

He pulled into the parking lot and made his way to the

back of the store. The old man running the cash register had barely paid him any mind. He didn't even acknowledge the door chime when Jeremiah stepped inside.

Once Jeremiah was in the bathroom, he unzipped his pants and tried to pee into the bowl without touching himself. The long ride in the truck, combined with his tight pants, had made that impossible. He had to reach into his zipper to aim.

After he finished, he turned on the hot water tap. He waited, trying not to think about the filth on his fingers. The steam began to build up from the sink. He placed his hand under the near-boiling water and let the pain cleanse him. With wet hands, he pressed the pump for the soap. It was empty.

*Now what, Janet?*

His heart beat harder in his chest. He needed soap or Mother would be displeased. She only called him "Janet" when he was in trouble.

"I'm sorry, Mother. I'll scrub as hard as I can."

He ground his hands together under the steaming water. His fair skin became red, but still, he rubbed harder.

"Must get rid of the evil."

He rubbed his hands together until he couldn't feel

the water anymore. They had become numb from too much pain.

*What did I tell you about touching yourself?*

"I wasn't, Mother. I needed to pee."

*Don't use that foul language in front of your Mother! You know my poor heart cannot handle such things.*

Jeremiah fell to his knees. His hands were still above him in the sink under the cascading water. Calmly, he took in a long slow breath, sucking it between his teeth.

"You're alright, Jeremiah."

He breathed out even slower than when he breathed in.

"Get a grip."

His heart rate started to slow and the twisting knot in his stomach began to loosen. Grasping the side of the sink, he pulled himself back up. As he turned off the water, he watched himself in the mirror. The steamed covered glass didn't allow him to take in his entire face, but he could at least get the idea that he was good enough to leave the bathroom.

The attendant yelled at him as he left the gas station. Jeremiah wasn't really paying attention, though. The man said something about the bathroom being for paying customers only. Jeremiah stopped and slowly turned to look at the man. His fists were clenched, and the color was starting to get back into his fingers. Jeremiah had no time to deal with petty issues. There must have been an obvious challenge on his face because the attendant faltered and went back to the magazine he had been reading.

*That's my boy.*

Once outside of the gas station, he was drawn to a white sedan that had pulled up to one of the gas pumps. There was nothing particularly interesting about it except that it had a green stripe running down the length of it, a little off from center. He hadn't seen a family-type sedan painted like a racing car before. But once the driver stepped out to feed her credit card into the gas pump, Jeremiah could see that the car fit her.

The driver's long frizzy blonde hair was pulled back in a fruitless attempt at a ponytail. Hayfield didn't have that much humidity, but the little that it did have was enough to send her hair into a tornadic mess. Her features were soft and round, but she was not overweight, from what Jeremiah could see.

She was looking at the machine, tapping in her information allowing to see a nice profile of her face. Her jaw was curved, and her plump cheeks almost hid her tiny nose. Her lips were pursed in concentration, but even so, they were full and painted to look like a bright purple plum. They looked so soft and inviting that they reminded Jeremiah of pillows. Then it hit him. She was the one.

*No! Look at her. She is filthy, Jerry. I will not allow this. I forbid it!*

He took his time getting back to his truck, measuring her from the corner of his eye. She was taller than the last ones - he estimated about six feet - just a few inches shorter than him. The way her dress was cut it made it look like she had disproportionately short legs. It was as if her height was made up by an abnormally long torso. He had not seen that body type before. She was so different; he was sure she was the one.

*That woman is dirt. She is filth. Listen to me.*

He shook his head and climbed into his truck. Safe in the cab, Jeremiah used the side mirror to see how his new friend was doing. She finished pumping gas and went to get back into the car. She stopped and looked down, looking for something. When she bent over to pick up whatever it was, his stomach tingled at the sight of her curves.

*You are dirty and your thoughts are unclean. Do not touch her, Janet.*

"Stop it, Mother!"

He slammed his head against the steering wheel. The shock to his forehead was familiar. His head rang, but the throb was soothing. Slowly, he rubbed his temples in deep circles. The throbbing ceded and he looked back in is a mirror to see more of his new friend. He cursed his luck. She had already left the gas station, and he didn't even know which direction she drove off to.

Jeremiah looked at himself in the rearview mirror. He licked his thumb and brushed a loose strand of hair in his brow.

"Maybe she's just going to freshen up for our date."

*Why are you doing this? These women are so unclean. All you need is your mother.*

"No! Leave me alone." He raged at his steering wheel.

*Jeremiah Adam Black! Do not talk to your mother that way!*

He flinched at his middle name. It was a constant reminder of how inferior he was. She had told him when he was a young boy that when he was born, she wanted to name him Adam. He had been her first son, so she wanted to name him after the first man.

But she decided against it. She said it hadn't felt right. And, as he grew up she would tell him that she was glad she hadn't given him the name. She said the real Adam was pure and perfect. He was not deserving of that name.

"If only…" he whispered under his breath.

He blinked back any more memories that threatened to plague him and left the parking lot. Taking a right, he drove just a few miles under the speed limit down the road, scanning for her green-striped car.

Jeremiah wasn't even sure which way the lady had gone but his mother had always told him: "follow the right hand of God and you will always make the right decisions." A stop light hindered his progress. He looked to see if he could find any trace of his curvaceous frizzy-headed lady. Instead, he spotted McLean Funeral Home.

He smiled and drove home to get his grandfather's suit. He always kept it cleaned and pressed in case he needed to impress a special lady. He knew it was out of fashion, but he liked it and people assumed it was "retro."

He would still need to wash his face and maybe put a little cream in his hair. There was plenty of time. In the employee parking lot on the right side of the funeral home was a shiny white car with a green stripe.

# CHAPTER SIX

The empty caskets lined the walls like murals in an art museum. Their glossy candy-coated exterior shined brightly in the dull light. Melissa never quite understood why people put so much thought and effort into picking them out. The price alone made her queasy.

They had models that ranged in quality; the most luxurious with their silk linings and gold plated accents and some even had special filling for the utmost comfort. When she had read that one, she had to take her lunch break to control her laughing. Didn't people know that these boxes were going to be put in the ground?

But Melissa didn't have to understand. Since working at the funeral home, she faced a wide range of emotions from people forced to choose how their loved ones spent eternity. She knew that this last purchase, one last gift of their love, allowed them closure. People needed closure, so she felt no shame in helping them choose the ones that they could barely afford. In her mind, she was helping people.

It was near closing time when Melissa noticed the old boxy pickup truck roll into the parking lot. It wasn't one of the new monsters that were built for glamour and status. The edges were straight and the lines were sharp. The recently shined hood was sun faded. It was taken care of; still a classic. It was a machine of simple strength, old elegance. So was the driver.

She figured the man that stepped out of the truck was only in his forties, but she couldn't tell. His face was hard but even from here she could see a glint in his eyes. His body was big, but not flashy. His broad, muscular shoulders weren't from time in front of a mirror, they were the shoulders of a man who worked with his hands. She smiled; a woman can always tell the difference.

When he closed the door to his truck, he looked at himself in the reflection in his window and ran his fingers through his fawn-colored hair. So light it was almost transparent, but the tips caught the setting sun and glowed orange, almost like a halo made of fire.

As he walked towards the front door, she studied his face from inside her office. She was trying to gather a preview of his emotions. There were no tears in his eyes, nor red cheeks, instead his skin was pale and his eyes were focused. It was a look of determination. She turned to the mirror to adjust herself.

She wanted to be prepared, both physically and mentally. Some family members came in so full of grief from their recent loss that they barely were able to make the final decisions for their loved ones. Those were the hardest. She didn't own this place; she was just in sales. It was just her job to make money. But these poor people sometimes needed a shoulder, not a sale.

Then there were the people that came in stone-faced, almost relieved. Whoever they were there for had been in pain or had suffered too long. Their death had been a relief and this was the final hurdle to get past it. These were the best. She felt like she was helping these people. The process was almost therapeutic for them and for her. It was just a bonus she made her greatest commissions on these cases. Mr. Pickup Truck looked like the latter kind.

She rebuttoned her blouse, she unbuttoned it after the

last customer left so that she could relax. The plain white fabric accented her natural curves, nearly busting at the seams. The busting seams, the white cotton, gave the impression of big soft pillows that a grieving widower could lay his head on for comfort. She thought it funny how some other women would unbutton their blouses to lure men into big sales. Her last husband had found comfort on them after picking out the casket for his late wife.

A soft chime rang through the building as the man stepped into the front parlor. She waited a few moments before walking out to greet him. He stood in the center of the parlor like he was waiting for her. She shook the thought away. Working at this place could spook anyone.

Mr. Pickup's long arms were hanging meekly by his side but there was a palpable strength to his presence. As she got closer, there was a slight scent coming from him. It reminded her of the pool. He was a few inches taller than she was, just tall enough that she had to look up into his eyes.

They were large, full of emotion, passion, and intelligence. They were a light brown to the point that they looked nearly golden. They were almost perfect except for one minor flaw. The pupil, impossibly dark, without any shine, was not a circle. They were rounded on top but as she followed them down the black jutted out through the iris and touched the whites. They reminded her of upside-down tears.

She must have been staring too long because the man spoke first.

"Good evening, Miss." His raspy, yet silky soft voice greeted her.

"Good evening, sir, my name is Melissa. How may I help you?"

"Well, Miss, my wife passed away recently. I want to get her the final resting place she deserves."

He fiddled with his hands as his eyes tried not to look her over. She knew that look well; she was quite proud of her figure.

"I'm sorry to hear that, but we here are happy to help to provide the very best resting place for your late wife." He smiled and she continued. "I'm sorry sir, I didn't catch your name." She placed her hand on his strong and solid arm to comfort him and kept it there. He stumbled a bit at her question, or at her touch. She wasn't sure which.

"Yes. Well, call me Jerry. Please." His smile widened, exposing a full set of teeth.

Bright and straight, the canines triggered something in

the back of her mind. They were slightly too long, but she dismissed any misgivings. He had a few irregularities. but nothing she couldn't get past. This man showed some promise.

She trailed her hand down his sleeve and grabbed one of his fidgeting hands. His fingers wrapped her hand in a vice-like grip. She winced in surprise.

She moved around so that she was next to him. Gently, she guided him to the showroom. Out of the corner of her eye, she noticed he wasn't watching where they were going, his eyes were trained on her. She felt as if she was being studied, sized up. He sure was strange. She ignored the nagging in the back of her mind. Her former husband's money was starting to run thin. She knew this one would be an easy catch.

***

Melissa sat at her desk, closing out the books for the night. She had made two sales. One just an hour or so ago to Mr. Pickup. That handsome Jerry had bought a top of the line casket, without much convincing. His disregard for the high price tag confirmed what she had suspected: he was from old money. That would explain his homely looks. New money was flashy and loud, old money was subdued and quiet.

Her first sale was to a lady in her upper nineties. She was burying her husband and was worried about the price. She didn't want to cremate him, but she couldn't have afforded a shoe box on her benefits. Melissa felt sorry for the old lady. Her name had been Patricia and she reminded her of her own grandmother.

She even smelled like her grandmother. It was a comforting mix of baby powder and spicy perfume. Patricia had spent almost the entire time talking about her late husband. They had been married for over sixty years. It was a beautiful story and Melissa didn't have the heart to try to sell her something she couldn't afford.

The funeral home had a fund set away for such occasions. The only stipulation was that it had to be one of the most basic models. The owner, Mr. McLean, had grown tired of seeing poor old grieving family members unable to pay one last respect to their family. Instead, he had set up a sort of piggy bank some time ago before Melissa started working there. Thanks to that fund, Mrs. Patricia could afford a final resting place for her husband. It made Melissa feel good.

She saved her progress and logged out of her computer account. She was the last employee there. Mr. McLean often left early, around four, to be with his grandkids and had been leaving her in charge for the remainder of the business day. She liked that just fine.

Besides, Mr. McLean knew what she was doing. He had to, and she figured he didn't want to be there when she was doing it. She had married her last husband only a few weeks after he came for help picking out a casket for his late wife. Normally, she did not pick up men under eighty, but even in his fifties, Mr. Hawthorne was not in good health. He only lasted about a year and a half, which was record time for her.

Jerry was also much younger than her normal catch. He was less than twenty years her senior, but the eyes had gotten her to thinking. She had read something about pupil abnormalities before, and she thought she remembered it being a bad sign. Besides, if his money was as old as she thought, it would be well worth the investment. It would only take a few dates with him to find that out.

Melissa pushed back from her desk and opened the top drawer. She dug out her keys and left her office, turning off all the lights. The dull orange street lamp on the corner glowed softly to light her exit.

There was a rumbling outside the building and she sighed. They had been closed for almost thirty minutes, well past any grace period for new customers. Besides, it was Friday night and she wanted to go home and relax. There was an unopened bottle of wine on the counter with her name on it. Then the door rattled.

Whoever had pulled up was trying to come in through the locked door. She hesitated. They were still trying to get in. She wondered if this may not be a customer. Then the rattling stopped. Peeking through the thick curtains over the glass window to the side of the door, there was a dark outline of some vehicle, but the shadows were too harsh for her to make it out. There didn't appear to be anyone in front of the door.

"Did I…"

Quickly turning in the pale orange light, she rushed to the back of the building, through the shadows as quickly as she could manage. She couldn't remember locking the back door.

The light was disappearing as she got closer the back of the building. Her hands groped the unfamiliar walls for another light switch, but she didn't spend much time back there.

Her fingers clawed at the wallpaper, looking for any source to fight back the black shadows. The darkness receded as she turned the corner. There was a soft white light from the full moon peeking into the hall; right through the open back door.

"Who's there?" She asked the shadows.

She waited with baited breath. There was no answer. As she took one cautious step after another, her blood pumped through her body at breakneck speed. The darkness engulfed her as she reached for the door and looked out. There was no sign of anything. She pulled the door close, the latch clicking softly into place and turning the deadbolt. Her hands trailed the wall; as she turned her fingers knocked the light switch.

The white-blue fluorescent light nearly blinded her. She rubbed the sight back into them; finally, able to blink past the bright light. The empty hall extended in front of her.She tried to calm herself, telling herself that she was being silly.

She walked back down the hall to the front door, trying to calm her unsettled mind. It was obviously some honest mistake about their hours. The back door was obviously just a coincidence. She must have left it open when she needed a breather earlier. *I must have, didn't I?* She couldn't remember closing it behind her so that must have been it.

She nodded as if that settled it. At the end of the hall, she found the other light switch that she hadn't been able to find earlier. She made one last look behind her at the door. It was still locked. *Nothing to worry about.* She hit the switch and turned back to the parlor. In the room under the pale orange glow from street lamp stood a figure, with its vice-like grip wrapped around her neck.

# CHAPTER SEVEN

Jeremiah stood in front of the mirror with the safety razor under the water. The hot cascade rinsed away the white foam and flakes of five o'clock shadow. He hadn't shaved since that morning, and the stubble had gotten a bit rough. He wanted to look his best for Melissa.

He had chosen her at the first meeting, but only on instinct. But after she had flirted with him at the funeral home, despite his story about the untimely death of his "wife," he had felt a connection. She was so shameless.

"They are nothing like you, Mother." He said to his reflection.

Once the razor was clean, he placed it in its holder and slapped on a little bit of spicy cologne he had picked up at the drugstore months ago. Mother would have been upset, but his tingling skin invigorated his feeling of defiance. When he picked it out, he didn't care what it smelled like. He had been eyeing the bottle since he was a boy and it hadn't changed in all those years. The little red ship on the label called to him.

He asked her to buy it for him once, but she had refused. Mother had always said that perfumes were for whores and that it was the same for cologne. She would never raise a man-whore.

His mother never even wore anything, just a fog around her full of the stinging smell of lye soap gently masked by baby powder. The heat made her sweat, especially as she had gotten older. She was constantly applying powder to cover the heat rashes, made worse by her diabetes. At the time, he did not know what she had; it was only as an adult he could figure it out.

"Oh no, I see you."

He grabbed the pair of small whisker scissors next to the razor and snipped a stray hair coming off his right eyebrow. This was their first date and he would not have anything out of place for her.

"Melissa."

Steam appeared on the mirror as her name escaped his lips. He liked her name. He wasn't quite sure why, but it seemed to fit her slightly shorter stature and curvy figure.

*A harlot if I have ever seen one, Jerry.*

He put down the scissors and left the bathroom. His warm house began to make his skin clammy, and he was glad he had left his clothes in his room. He was not the best at doing laundry, so he always left them upstairs so that his date would not mess them up. Another lesson he had learned the hard way with the first one.

His first date had been such a debacle. After his mother's death, Jeremiah had been in a haze. Days passed without direction or purpose. For his whole life, she had been there to guide him and show him what to do. He was not equipped to be a self-sufficient man. But just like that, he was required to be one.

He had seen his first one downtown. The resemblance was so striking he almost called her "Mother" multiple times during his introduction. In retrospect, she wasn't anything like his mother, but, when stricken with grief, the mind plays many tricks.

It didn't matter, though. The resemblance was enough – or his mind was far enough gone – that she became the object of his new obsession. He learned that her name was Haley. They had gone out for coffee that night. It was nice, at first.

But whatever physical traits reminded him of his mother, that's where the similarities ended. She cursed constantly. Jeremiah had to fight the urge to stuff his fingers in his ears to block out her foul language. She did not believe in having children or starting a family. Even worse, she was agnostic.

He found all this out when she had allowed him to walk her home from the coffee shop. They were a few blocks away when something came over him. Haley was not Mother, but he needed her to be. He needed an outlet for all the sadness and rage he had been feeling. In the middle of the street, the only witness the orange sulfur lamp, he strangled her.

Through his fog of sadness and rage, he knew enough that he had left evidence on her. Since he couldn't leave her there, he brought her to his house. If he could thank his upbringing for only one thing, it was teaching him how to clean. That's when he realized it would just be easier to bring them to his basement first. It was at the door to the basement that he now stood, once again, for his date.

He opened the lock on the large sliding bolt, keeping the thick oak door closed. He undid the combination to the second lock on the top corner and pulled out the metal pin. On the third lock on the bottom corner, he entered the combination but it wouldn't open. This lock was always trouble, but he could not bring himself to replace it.

It was the lock from his date with Haley. When he had tied her up, he couldn't find anything to keep her from rolling around. He got the bright idea to bend her arms back and lock them to the ties around her feet. It wasn't pretty, but it was effective. Now the lock was old, and despite his best attempts to keep it clean and well lubricated, the accumulation of fluids and bleach had warped the tumblers.

It finally gave way as everything always did. His tall stature, much taller than he could have inherited from his mother, lent him great strength. Not much could resist it. The door couldn't resist him, either, and it slid open on large steel hinges. He had replaced those some time ago. The original ones were rusty and very brittle.

He reached into the darkness and turned on the light. The warm orange glow lit the steps. The half lighting made him feel shrouded and protected during the first few moments of their meeting in this new situation. He saved the bright lights for when he felt more confident. She was so pretty; his confidence wasn't up to par just yet.

*Look at you, giddy with your unholy temptation. Try not to soil yourself with this one.*

He closed the door behind him and placed the large metal arm over it, locking it into grooves on the door frame. This was his first expense when reconditioning his parlor. He had been about to remove the marks his fingers left on Haley's neck and, at the time, the door only locked from the kitchen side. That's when a nosey lady handing out leaflets nearly interrupted him.

On accident, he had left his front door cracked open through the night when he had returned home with her. He had spent so much time downstairs enjoying her cold body, that he didn't realize the moon had gone down and the sun had come back up. The lady had seen the open door and poked her head in and called out.

It wasn't her fault really, he admitted to himself. The neighborhood was old and people were too comfortable there. He bet she had been let in and talked to by countless of other houses on his street. When he heard her call, he ran upstairs.

His naked body had caught the lady off-guard.

Luckily, she didn't think anything odd about it. Extremely embarrassed, she left without a word. It was just as well. He was already on a date, and she wasn't his type. Even so, if she made a fuss she would have been included. That evening, he went out and bought a barricade.

He whistled the small melody he had learned as a child as he went downstairs. It was only comprised of the same six notes, repeated over and over but at different octaves. To him it was soothing, the melody wrapped itself around him like a security blanket. But to his dates, the tune came off as ominous, foreboding. None of them enjoyed it as much as he did. When he came to the foot of the stairs, Melissa was sobbing.

"Please, let me go," she cried.

He had removed the gag from of her mouth when he brought her into the house. Even though he had knocked her out at the funeral home, he had wanted to gag her just in case she came to. Her voice soothed him. He almost wished she would talk to him while he worked instead of just screaming.

"I will, I promise. You will leave here."

He smiled and reached out with one hand to pat the top of her head. She snapped to the side, exposing her teeth.

He was quick and her teeth smashed together on nothing but the air. Laughter filled the air, he was used to it. She might have gotten him if he hadn't been looking at her from the corner of his eye.

He still couldn't look at her naked body directly, shy to the end. Even when he had stripped her before locking her to the table, he made sure to keep his eyes closed.

Gently, he used his hands to find his way across her skin. Always the gentleman, he even made sure to not let her head bang as he sat her down on the cold steel medical table.

The table was in the middle of the parlor room of the basement, where most of his dates started and ended. Across from the table to the right of the room was his desk and cabinets, all made of polished steel. He had made the change after Haley when he realized wooden furniture was impossible to clean. Steel was the only thing strong enough to stand up to the sanitizing.

In the main storage area, he ran his fingers over the peeling labels on the shelves. *Such a disgrace.* They weren't particularly old, but the humidity in the basement had destroyed the adhesive. He needed to replace them before they were too difficult to read.

He snorted when he finally found the bottle he was

searching for. Gabbing the little vial of fentanyl and a syringe, he stuck the latter into the former and pulled the stopper filling it. He turned to Melissa; she was staring daggers at the filled syringe in his hand.

"Thank you for coming, Melissa. You're very pretty," he said.

She swallowed as if she was trying to come to a hard decision. He didn't know what she could be thinking about. It wasn't as if she had a choice about what he was doing to her.

"Please, you don't have to do this, you know? I can do whatever you need. You don't have to hurt me."

She arched her back against the restraints, pushing her breast into the shadows. Jeremiah laughed, the echoes bouncing around the room. Her back slapped against the steel table; defeated in her attempt. He knew what she was doing. They didn't all act the same, but some of the women tried to seduce him into letting his guard down so they could escape. He had fallen for that once, too, but never again.

None-the-less, he held a little more respect for Melissa. She deserved the fentanyl. He hated to see women suffer. This didn't have anything to do with them, really, and he knew that inside. That's why he got them the drugs. This was about another woman.

He placed the needle on her arm and pressed in. She let a harsh gasp and a slight scream. Forcing the clear liquid into her body, he pressed the plunger all the way in.

"Shhh, Melissa, stay calm, let it work."

He smiled, laid the syringe down on his desk, and placed the vial back in the cabinet. He wiped his hands on the bleach-soaked cloth that was hung on a nail in the wall.

"Please. Please, Jerry. Why?"

She pressed against her restraints, pleading for mercy. He didn't know why she didn't see that he had given her mercy in the form of the fentanyl. Had he wanted her to suffer, he would have skipped that step. But women were vessels. No matter what, they were vessels.

*There was only one pure woman, and even she succumbed to the evil temptation.*

"Jerry, please…" A slur crept into her words as the medicine started to work.

"Quiet down, sweetheart, you have been a bad girl."

He leaned down and grabbed her right hand. Her small, soft fingers were painted red and they shined even in the low light of the basement. He let the hand fall to the metal table and turned back to his desk of tools, picking up the sheers that had once been one of the gardening tools left in the house.

When he turned, Melissa saw what he had in his hand. She let out a muffled scream, but the fentanyl was too strong. He may have given her a tad too much.

*Oh, well, hopefully, it'll last longer and not wear off halfway through like it did for one unfortunate date.*

He grabbed her delicate hand in his again and examined it. Her short slender fingers looked delicate like a candied flower. He wrapped his lips around her middle finger and took a slow, long, suck, letting her sweat born of her fear mix with his saliva born of desire.

He could feel the fingertip twitching in his mouth as she tried to fight the fentanyl, but the high dose was making her too groggy. He slipped the finger out of his mouth and smiled at her.

*She is such a dirty soul.*

"Yes, Mother." He said and stroked the back of Melissa's hand.

*Cleanse her, those hands have been foul.*

"Yes, Mother."

He kissed the back of her hand, he didn't want to scare her, he just wanted to make her life better. *Why couldn't she see that?* Like an eagle swooping down on rats in the field, the garden shears swooped in and cut off the middle three fingertips. They fell to the table, her shiny nails clinked on the steel as they bounced once and settled.

Jeremiah reveled in the look in her eyes. She could see it; she knew what had happened. Her mind wanted to scream, to know the pain so it could fight back. But her mind couldn't understand the lack of feeling. It was too far away from her consciousness and all she could do was cry.

Streams of red flew and splattered on his thigh. It dribbled down the front of his leg and wrapped around his knee, falling in small droplets on the floor. He couldn't help but think of how womanly he looked.

*I guess I have the curse, too.* He thought with a slight giggle.

He closed his eyes and enjoyed the warmth spilling down his leg, a memory flooded back to him. When he was six, he was supposed to be studying his Scriptures. He had placed a bookmark in the Bible and gotten up to go pee. They had three bathrooms in their small house. One was only for his mother and it was upstairs in her room. He also had a small toilet in his room.

The one that he used that day was the guest bathroom. He never knocked on the door before entering since it was only the two of them. She only ever used her own washroom. Except for this time.

He wished he had been old enough to understand what was happening at the time. Looking back, he knew now that she had been in the process of changing her sanitary napkins and was disposing of the old one. Eventually he would find out this was perfectly normal; however, the six-year-old Jeremiah knew nothing of those things. Instead, he screamed for the health of his mother.

"Mother! You're hurt! Let me call the doctor!"

Had he left it there it wouldn't have been as bad, but she was hurt. So, as any good son would do, he rushed to comfort her. As he wrapped his arms around her soft frame, his arm grazed the soiled napkin in her hand. It smeared a dark maroon stain across his arm.

"You are filthy! Look at that mess! Get out of here, Janet!"

She tossed the trash in her hand and grabbed Jeremiah by the back of the collar. Her eyes flickered and became clouded. The white fog from her developing cataracts disappeared. Her eyes became black swirls of emptiness, and he felt a void in his heart. She lifted him up with unimaginable strength and placed him in the bathtub.

She turned the hot water tap on full power, making him stand under it until he could feel the familiar burn. As the steam started to rise from his wet clothes, she rummaged under the sink and pulled out the white plastic bottle. She grabbed a ball of steel wool and poured the bleach over the bundle of fibers shining in her palm.

As the blood ran down his thigh, they collected slightly in the small scars that she had given him that day. The lessons she had taught were always with him.

He looked back at Melissa. Her skin paled as her fingers dripped. She was losing blood too fast. He sighed. He hated using the brand, but he needed to burn the wounds closed so she didn't bleed out.

They still had the rest of their date.

# CHAPTER EIGHT

Jeremiah undid the restraints that held Melissa to the table. She was having a hard time moving, and he didn't think that she posed any risk of getting away.

Melissa's breath began to slow back down to normal as the shock of seeing her fingers cut short began to wear off. Her speech was less slurred, but the fentanyl was still pumping through her system, keeping the pain at bay. Her tone was pathetic as she continued to beg for his humanity. But Jeremiah had been humane. He had taken her pain away.

"Jerry… please… Jerry…" She moaned as she tested the open restraints.

"Shhh, Melissa."

He placed a finger on her lips. He was struck by how

velvety and firm they were. They reminded him of the felted teddy he had when he was younger, soft and inviting. He bent down and placed his lips just above hers, her breath escaping her lovely lips and entering his body. He was breathing her life in. He placed his lips on hers.

*Do not touch my son, whore!*

Jeremiah recoiled as the scream rang in his mind. He had soiled himself with her filthy lips.

"It wasn't my fault, Mother, she lured me in. I was innocent."

*I saw you. You are just as dirty as she is.*

"No, Mother, I'm not. She won't be able to tempt me again."

He turned on his heels, dropping the garden shears on the table next to Melissa. Returning to his desk of tools, he pulled the middle drawer open and rummaged through the contents. Towards the back, he found it: a little black box.

Pulling it out, he clicked the small snap on the side, exposing the silver rod with the sharp thin razor blade on the end. He had other scalpels, real scalpels, but this one was special, he had made when he was sixteen. He turned back to Melissa. He needed to take away her weapons. He was not expecting to see her sitting up on the edge of the table, wielding the shears.

She had managed to wrap her mangled fingers around them after he had dropped them. He cursed his stupidity and made a mental note to chastise himself later. Somehow, she managed to push herself into a propped-up position, although she hadn't the strength to get off the table yet. The shears were pointed at him.

"Let...me...go..."

Jeremiah could see her body was fighting through the chemicals in her blood. That was a good thing. As they wore off, the pain from her fingers would begin to rise. He knew he could just wait her out. But he shook his head. He couldn't just let her suffer like that. She was a victim. She was a victim of her own life.

"Melissa, darling-"

"No!" She managed a scream, and she pushed the shears towards him. Jeremiah didn't know if she thought he was closer than he was, or if her eyes were blurry from the medications, but her violent thrust didn't produce even a feeble attempt at his life. She fell off the table. Her head made a funny little crunch that Jeremiah wished he could have recorded and played repeatedly.

She had not been knocked out, she was still looking at

him, but she wasn't moving much. He stepped towards her and gazed at the ground. He didn't think there was a real need to pick her up and put her on the table. *She's just fine down there.*

He knelt beside her and opened her eyes the rest of the way. Streaks of red radiated through her whites like little cracks. He grabbed her chin and placed a kiss on her soft painted lips. He smiled into her mouth, and a sigh escaped his lips. He was always so nervous on with the first kiss, but the second was much better. He loved the taste of her lipstick.

*How dare you, Janet. You filthy, filthy little boy.*

"No, Mother, we are on a date. It's okay."

*You are such an embarrassment. You soiled yourself once again! I bet you are messing your britches, too. Filth!*

"No! I'm sorry Mother!"

He covered his eyes with his hand. He didn't want his date to see his tears. Through the gaps in his fingers, he could see Melissa's head trying to turn.

*Is she looking for an escape? Why doesn't she want to be with me, Mother?*

*No one wants to be with you, Jerry.*

Melissa's face twitched. The drugs were wearing off,

and the pain from her fingers was starting to seep into her consciousness. Her lips curled. The sneer was born from pain. But Jeremiah didn't know that. All he saw was a smile.

*She's laughing at me!*

He reached out with his homemade scalpel and pulled the blade through her bottom lip. It fell from her face like an orange peel.

*She's laughing at you, Jerry.*

He removed her upper lip just as easily. His blade was sharp; it was his pride and joy. He stood up and placed the scalpel on the desk where it would wait until he was ready to clean it.

He wiped his eyes and turned back to his date. Her face was obscured by the mess she had made. But his eyes were being pulled away. In her struggle and her fall, her chest was pushed to the floor and her hips were thrust up into the air. He licked his lips hungrily.

*Mother will be so mad.*

# CHAPTER NINE

The steam carried the bleach into his nostrils, and he breathed the relaxing fumes in deeply. The water was just a little less than boiling and it felt good on his naked skin. He sat in the tub, scrubbing away the dried blood from under his fingernails. The steel wool stung as he dug in, but not as much as when he had to clean his dirty place.

Mother warned him to never let a woman touch him down there. She wouldn't even say its name – he found out that it was called a *penis* from a television show. After that, she had broken the set with the leg of one of the kitchen chairs.

He couldn't help himself. Melissa was just there, and their date was going so well. He wasn't sure if he was good enough for her, he had only been with four women before, and they had not complained. But, just like Melissa, when he removed their womanly parts afterward so that he could clean them; they complained.

"I'm just trying to clean them, Mother. Why do they cry so?" He asked the wad of steel wool in his hands. The grey fibers were stained red; he would have to throw it away soon.

He dunked his head under the surface of the water. Letting the heat and bleach work their way into his face and scalp, he needed to remove all traces of what he had done. He hated that no one understood his love for these women. He was making them better. Other men just used them for filthy pleasure, and then they left them with their dirty seed. His love was cleansing.

Melissa had become unresponsive after he did *what he did*. He needed to clean her, and she didn't even scream when he placed her in the steel basin. He had installed it in the back for the Letting Room.

There was a large heating coil under the steel basin. After he placed her in the barely warm water, he turned the dial on the coil to full power. He left her in there for just under ten minutes.

When he pulled her out, her skin was shiny and pink. She was so beautiful; he was glad that he didn't have to dismember her anymore for her to fit in his duffel bag. He folded her once over her stomach and placed her with care in the duffle bag, along with the plastic bag of extra parts. Then that he decided to take his own bath.

Afterwards, he stood up in the tub, the water dripped from his body like the droplets off of a stalactite. They plopped on the surface, slightly echoing against the tile walls. Their little ripples were like waves in the ocean and they crashed together around his feet.

He stepped out of the tub and picked up a towel. Wrapping it around his face, he breathed in the smell. The harsh vinegar made the towels that much softer.

In his quest to be as clean as his mother, the first time he had soiled himself with a woman he had drawn himself a hot bleach bath. For good measure, he added a cup of vinegar to the bath water.

To him, if both were good on their own, then together they would be even more powerful. She had not told him any different before she died. That night he learned a hard lesson, and he never did it again.

He shook away the memory and toweled off the rest

of his body. He went to his room to pick out clothing. His wardrobe was sparse, but he dressed in his "going out" clothes. His grandfather's jeans fit him and he wore them often. They had been thoroughly worn through the seat and crotch from years of wearing and washing.

He pulled out a red and blue striped button-up shirt. This was the last gift his mother had given him before she died. He hadn't received a present for his birthday ever since.

He slid his long arms through the soft sleeves. Then, glanced in the mirror to make sure the collar was buttoned down, and then he tucked the tails into his waistline. He ran his thumbs from above the fly, and pushed it around his stomach, gathering all the fabric in the back so that he looked dapper if he did say so himself.

The one piece of clothing, an accessory really, that he had bought himself was the black leather belt. It had embroidered seams around the edge that came together in a small fleur-de-lis at the edge of the buckle. The bright silver face of the buckle was broad and had a small gold cross on it. It was flashy, but for the right reasons.

He had bought the belt after her death. His grandfather's belt carried too many memories of lashings across his bare backside. If he had been exceptionally bad, his grandfather's belt found him across the top of his thighs. Only once did it ever find his face.

As he pulled his shoes on, his face stung with the memory of that night. He knew it was his fault; he had bought a forbidden item from the store. He was not supposed to buy comic books, and he normally never had the money to buy them either. His mother didn't trust him with money, so she had a tab at the store that she would pay off once a month.

On his way to the store, he had found a dollar bill in the grass. He almost hadn't seen it. It had been rolled up tight, and there was something that looked like baby powder on the edge. He had thought it was fake at first, he had never seen money like that, but when he unrolled it, the portrait of the old white-haired man looked back up at him. It was real.

At the drug store, he picked out the few items that she had sent him to buy: bread, milk, and sugar. That was breakfast every morning. She would have a tall glass of milk with a few spoonsful of sugar swirled in with a side of toast. Sometimes, she would even dunk the toast into the milk. After he picked up her necessities, he wandered around.

He was looking for something to spend his dollar on. He walked down the sweets aisle and thought that he could buy a bag of candy. He had never had Skittles, but their beautiful shiny shells were so enticing.

He often lingered next to them on other shopping trips. He thought about buying a bag of M&M's but they were crunchy and hard to clean off his teeth. He had been given them by the mailman on Christmas in the spirit of the holiday. When his mother saw his brown teeth, she doled out three lashings, one for each colorful candy he had eaten.

He continued to walk around the store when he came to the book aisle. He was not allowed to read many books, except for the Bible and sometimes the T.V. Guide. There were even a few newspaper articles that passed her scrutiny, and he got to read those – after she cut them out from the rest of the "sordid words."

He was about to by-pass the aisle when he saw it. It was brightly colored and glossy and had been placed directly under the buzzing fluorescent light. The cover beckoned him like a lighthouse down the aisle.

The mostly blue cover had a large red figure flying across the front. He had white eyes and black webbing across his body. It had huge yellow letters: "The Amazing Spider-Man."

He had never read a comic before because they were

printed by the Devil - per his mother. He had sometimes heard other kids mention Spider-Man before. They said how he was a hero and could do all sorts of things, but Jeremiah didn't know much else. The price on the cover said seventy-five cents. He had just enough.

When he returned home, he was careful as he put away the groceries. The comic was rolled around his calf and stuffed it into his sock, but the sock had started to fall. He was scared he was going to lose his new little treasure before he could get to his room and read it. After being dismissed, he ran upstairs. She wouldn't bother him for a least an hour. She was in the living room, busy crocheting a new hat for the winter.

Once in his room, he made his first mistake. He locked the door. The doors were not allowed to be locked in the house. She always said that if he had to hide what he was doing from her; God would still see and tell her. His second mistake was reading at his desk.

Pulling the book out of his sock, he climbed into his seat at the desk. He laid it down on, careful not to let it contact too hard. He felt like he was moving eggs around, and wanted to use the utmost care.

He turned on his table lamp and hunched over the old

worn wooden desktop. The pages had become a little damp from the sweat on his leg. He didn't care, this was his. *His.* It was finally something Mother hadn't provided for him. It was the first time he remembered feeling pride. Looking back, that should have been a clue that he was in the wrong. Pride is a sin, after all.

Sin or not, he marveled at the cover. This was most likely his last comic book, so he wanted to enjoy every little moment. Only using the very tips of his fingers, he turned the pages, careful to not let them tear. His eyes soaked in the beautiful lines. The drawings were so life-like, he could feel the hero swinging out on his spider webs.

After the first three pages, he needed to pee. The man in the book was so captivating, he had forgotten to go to the bathroom when he started. It was the way he talked about justice and truth, the strength, the power. It was the way the skin-tight suit showed off the muscles that Jeremiah wished he would have when he grew up.

He left the comic open to the page and went to the little bathroom attached to his bedroom. After he peed in the toilet, he washed his hands with a bar of homemade lye soap and scrubbed them with the steel wool.

He did this any time that he touched himself, even if it

was just to pee. His hands were still slippery from the soap when the bedroom door rattled.

"Jeremiah Adam Black! You open this door this instance. How dare you lock me out in my own home!"

*Oh no! Full name, need to hurry!*

He rubbed his hands under the hot water as hard as he could; trying to get the last traces of soap off. He heard footsteps retreat down the hall.

*Oh, no: Grandfather's belt.*

He rubbed harder until the skin shone and began to squeak. He dried them on the hand towel and went straight for the door. He turned the little silver button to the right, unlocking it just as she returned.

She stood in the doorway like a bear that had reared up on her hind legs. In one hand, she held a rag which she carried around to mop her forehead. Clenched in her other hand was the belt, the black leather was well worn from years of use. It was looped over so that she held both ends in her hands. He counted himself fortunate that she never hit him with the large studded buckle, even though she often reminded him how he didn't deserve that much leniency.

He hung his head in shame and turned to go to his bed. He would rest his elbows on the mattress for his punishment. Then he saw the incriminating evidence on his desk, open to the page he had stopped on. The scream from his mother told him that she had seen it too.

Something came over her, it was as if a black gossamer veil rose up from the floor and draped itself over her body. He only saw it briefly before she charged towards the desk. She grabbed the comic in the hand holding the rag. While balancing the belt in her other hand, she tore the comic down the spine.

"What kind of demonic trash have you brought into this house?" She screamed, as she doubled over the pages and ripped them down the middle again.

"Mother, no! Please!"

Jeremiah cried and scrambled to pick up the pieces of the book as they fell to the carpet. The air cracked and his hand turned red as the belt smacked across the top of it. He pulled his hand back, cradling it to his chest. Tears welled up in his eyes.

"How dare you talk back to me! How dare you bring this filth into this house! How dare you mock me with your existence, you evil little child!"

The last thing that Jeremiah remembered was the look in his mother's eyes. The hazel color had vanished and the black pupil had taken over each one. Even though she was looking at him, it felt like she didn't see him. Then the whole world went black, just like her eyes.

He didn't wake up until the next morning. He was in his pajamas, which he hadn't been in before, and was under the covers. Only one eye obeyed when he tried to open both eyes. When he went to the bathroom, there was a large red welt across his face extending from his lower draw, up across the swollen eye, to his temple.

He finished tying his shoe, and then let out a deep sigh. He had been holding his breath and didn't even realize it. He could almost feel the sting in his eye again, and he had to fight the urge to run to the mirror and check to make sure his face wasn't swollen. The memories hurt almost as much as the day it happened.

# CHAPTER TEN

He looked at his watch. There was less than an hour before the sun came up over the horizon. He needed to head out now, less the sunlight betray him. Downstairs, he slung the strap of the duffle bag over his head and placed it on the opposite shoulder. It helped distribute the awkward weight more evenly.

He took the bag to his truck and drove out to her house, less than thirty minutes away. He had found her address in her purse. It was only right to take her back home at the end of their date; like a gentleman. By the time he got there, the edge of the sun was just starting to peak over the dusty horizon.

He pulled into the empty driveway; her car was still at

the funeral home. Out of the truck, he looked around to see if anyone was waking up with their nose ready to be in other people's business. The neighborhood was still asleep; he felt confident enough to walk her to the doorstep like a true gentleman.

He placed the bag down on the doorstep and put on his gloves. He pulled out her head from inside and propped it against the threshold. She still smelled of bleach, but her skin had already started to lose its shiny red coloring in favor for a pasty white.

Next, he placed her fingertips by what was left of their respective fingers. He didn't know if they would need it to identify her - he wasn't sure how all that worked. But, he tried to make it easy for the police to treat her body with respect. They were sometimes so callous with his dates.

He placed her lips beside her on the threshold. He would have put them where they belonged, but he was worried they would fall off. He didn't want them to become lost before the police arrived.

He pulled out a plastic bag and held it close to his chest as a baby does their teddy. He wanted to keep it, he figured he could make something special out of it. But, this date hadn't been like the others. As the night worn on, he realized that she didn't have the same spark. Instead, he placed the freshly bleached uterus on Melissa's empty stomach. He had cleaned with extra precision to make sure they didn't find his filth still in it.

He sat in his truck and sighed as the engine roared to life. This night had not been what he wanted. He wanted to get home and take a nap before it got too late in the day.

Usually, he didn't take naps, but he had been up so late that he didn't get any sleep. He knew if he tried to function without enough rest, he could become a monster, which was not good.

# CHAPTER ELEVEN

Rachel picked up the box of off-brand feminine wash and placed it in her basket. She didn't normally come to Mr. Lipmann's, but she was heading home from her "date." She shuddered slightly, this one had been especially disgusting. Her breasts still felt grimy; he had kept twisting and turning them like they were doorknobs. But that wasn't nearly as bad as the feeling between her legs.

She couldn't just shower there and scrub it out. She didn't want him taking back his gifts, and she still had three semesters left to get her Bachelor's in Business. There was no way to keep her heavy schedule and a job at the same time.

She had already come to terms with using her

company to get men to pay for her college courses. Besides, she was almost a professional by now. There was a website that they could hire her to "escort" them to private functions.

As she walked down the aisle, she passed the large section of pads and tampons. She smiled, she hadn't had a period in nine years. Out of morbid curiosity, she grabbed a box of pads and considered the reflective wrapper.

On her thirteenth birthday, her mother talked to her about what to expect. The crying, the cramps, the spotting. She had told her that when the time came, to not be afraid and come to her with any questions. It was normal, it was natural, and it was a part of becoming a woman.

Rachel hadn't been worried about having her first period until her mom made a big deal about it. Her mom bought a box of pads from their drug store in Tallahassee, and she showed her how to unwrap and place it correctly. The box stayed under her bathroom sink for over a year.

It was October when it finally came. It would have been more fitting if it had waited until Halloween, but what happened to her made that Friday night of October 12th worse than any horror house she could have imagined.

They had just finished dinner; macaroni and cheese

with little, fried chunks of ham. There had been a side of spinach, but she had tossed it when her mother was feeding Rachel's baby brother.

About halfway through her meal, a sharp pain radiated from the top of her thighs. It reached up and wrapped around her stomach as if a snake were trying to rip through her belly button. She excused herself from the table and ran to her room. She barely made it before the first spill of warmth escaped her body.

Naked from her waist down, she sat on the edge of the bathtub. The small running shorts that she still had on after her track meet, and the poor pair of panties that had gotten in the way, were both in the trash can. Her mother had said "spotting," but it had been so much more.

She tried to clench to stop the flow. She didn't know if that was possible, but she tried anyway. It was still traveling down her legs, and the waves of stabbing pain were cutting into her back and sides with a fury.

Her hands gripped the safety bar as the crushing pain hit her body. In between the waves of agony, she had tried to call for her mother, but she was unable to catch her breath. She could barely do more let a river of tears cascade down her freckled cheeks.

Rachel had never been very religious. She had gone to Sunday School during elementary school and the first parts of the middle school. But when she had turned thirteen her mother had given her the option.

Like any teen, she didn't use any deep spiritual thoughts or beliefs to make her decision. Saturdays were track meets and practices, thus leaving Sunday as the only day to go to the movies with her girlfriends: Roxie and Hellen. There wasn't time to do anything else.

But at that moment, with the blood of her maturity pooling around her feet, she thrust herself on to her knees in the tub and crossed her chest with her fingers. She squeezed her eyes to the point they started to burn. She didn't want to see the crimson flood rippling with her tears. It had grown inexplicably deep. She must have been hallucinating this entire nightmare, she just wanted to wake up.

"God, it's me, Rachel Bliss. Please help…"

It felt like the inside of her stomach was ripped down the center, and her legs twitched under her thighs with pain. She didn't know what to expect from her first period, but this was not right. This was not how it was supposed to be, and she knew it.

"Please, God, help me. I'm scared." Tears fell between her legs.

Then she appeared.

Rachel never quite understood what happened after she prayed to God for help. She opened her eyes and saw a reflection in the pool of blood and tears between her knees. The face looking up was not hers.

Instead of Rachel's strawberry blonde hair flowing down her shoulders that ended in little curls over her chest, the reflection had jet black hair that curled up in a bob under her chin. And where Rachel had powder-blue eyes just like her father, the reflection had black eyes, no whites, no colored iris. Blank dark circles looked back at Rachel with a twisted little smile that made Rachel sick.

What happened next she tried to explain only once. The reflection stopped smiling and reached for her. The reflection *reached* for her through the surface of the shining blood beneath her legs. The black fingers slowly broke the surface towards her.

They wrapped around her narrow face and began to pull her down. Rachel pulled back against the black finger's grip on her face. She pushed against the sides of the tub and tried to stand up.

The lady was too strong. She tried one last time, jerking with her whole body. The reflection either let go or she lost her grip as Rachel flew backward. Her head cracked against the tile. Her whole world went black. Just like the Lady in the Blood's eyes.

Rachel woke up in the hospital to the doctor mumbling some pleasantries to her mother standing on the opposite side of her hospital bed. Her father wasn't there. The doctor gave Rachel the news when she came fully around.

There had been a complication within her reproductive tract that caused severe hemorrhaging in her uterus. The doctor said that the severe loss of blood had caused her to pass out and hit her head on the tile wall. But what was worse was what the doctor told her next. There was irreversible damage, she would not be able to have children.

Her mother cried for hours after the doctor left. Rachel didn't understand at the time why she was so upset. At fourteen, she was more interested in track and getting a scholarship to college. Rachel was not that upset at the news, not really. But her mother knew it would hit her eventually.

After her mother finally stopped crying, Rachel tried

to tell her about the Lady in the Blood. Her mother smiled, but it was not a happy one. It was the smile that an adult makes when they must tell their children bad news, and they are trying to mitigate the sadness.

"Honey, you've been through a terrible ordeal. You just hallucinated. The lack of blood, the hit to your head, that can all play tricks on your mind."

"But, Mom."

"Enough, Rachel!" she snapped. She recoiled at her own harshness and spoke softer. "We will schedule you an appointment with a doctor if you want." Her voice was calm, but her eyes begged to be tested.

Rachel had a sense about what kind of doctor her mom had been talking about. They were already in a hospital for her body. She assumed her mom was suggesting the kind for the head. She dropped anything else about the Lady in the Blood, and she never tried to speak of her again. Rachel knew she wasn't crazy.

As she grew up, when she saw the dull black eyes looking back at her, she ignored it. She ignored the eyes as they watched her lose her virginity from the back of the Jeep.

A year later, she ignored the eyes in the mirror while she cleaned up the blood on her hands. She had earned that blood when she lost control and beat her date without mercy. She broke his nose, along with his tooth, when he tried to push himself on to her.

The next nine years were spent pretending that the face didn't look back at her during her times of need and stress. Her mom must have been right, her mind just created shadows. It was obviously just the stress making her see those eyes. She never went to a doctor or told another person about it.

When she saw her reflection in the shiny plastic wrap around the box of pads in her hands, she made sure she didn't look too hard. Was it her blonde hair? She didn't care. She set the box down and left the aisle. There was one more thing to pick up, anyways.

# CHAPTER TWELVE

After Rachel grabbed the last item, she stood in the checkout line, munching on an open bag of Dots. She couldn't help it; they were her favorite candy. There was something about the gummy fruit flavors sticking to her teeth that made her happy. They reminded her of a long night of trick-or-treating with her younger brother, the colorful little wrappers spread across the floor like precious jewels pulled out of the earth.

There was an older lady in front of her talking to the clerk and they were taking longer than Rachel would have liked. Rachel didn't mind waiting, not really. The old lady reminded her of her Gran-Gran. She waited silently, wishing she could return to a childhood innocence.

Then the man came in. He walked in the door and waved to the clerk as if they knew each other. It wasn't like the movies, even though when he came in she did find it hard to catch her breath. But it wasn't "love at first sight" or any nonsense like that. It was more like a rollercoaster.

She found it odd, he wasn't attractive, nothing near a heartthrob. But he had a classically handsome face, the kind found in the black and white movies that her Gran-Gran watched. She couldn't remember the name of the actor she had loved, but she thought it was Clark.

The man was very tall, and she loved tall men. But just as fast as her first reaction, the attraction dissipated into the stale air of the little grocery store. There was something wrong. He looked as if he was draped in a shadow, despite the high sun flooding through.

As he turned left towards the cleaning supplies, he looked back and caught Rachel's stare. It was in his eyes that she lost it. It was a familiar feeling. Her vision became cloudy, blurring the world around her. She watched him walk down the aisle and pick up two bottles of bleach. Without realizing it, she smiled, and there was a feeling of pride that she could not explain.

Unblinking, she continued to follow him as he walked

to the back of the store and pick up a gallon of milk, then picked up a carton of eggs. She didn't even pretend not to watch his every move. She was so proud of him; he was such a grown little man and so handsome.

*Where did that come from?*

While she stared unabashedly at him as he shopped, he kept raising his eyes and sneaking a quick glance at her. She had that effect on men. It was the main reason she hadn't had to pay for a single hour of college credit. But as he kept throwing her looks, she realized it was different than looks of other men.

With every other man, she was used to them undressing her with their gaze, the gawks, as well as the looks of disgust and shame. Usually, the disgust was from her date's wives, and the shame was from the men who paid way more than she was worth. The men who had not been with their wives for the longest time always paid the most.

No, the look in his eyes was familiar without her having seen it before. It was almost like the look of recognition. It was the look of safety and love. She didn't know this man, but the strangest thought came to her, and she couldn't control it.

*My boy.*

# CHAPTER THIRTEEN

Jeremiah slumped down in the front seat of his truck, his face buried in his old copy of the King James Bible. He wasn't reading it; he didn't need too. He had almost memorized the whole book already. He was using it as a cover so that he could covertly watch her from the truck.

He had just finished picking up his normal groceries at Lipmann's. Gabriel was at the counter where he always was, talking to Mrs. Gloria. He couldn't ever remember Mrs. Gloria's last name, but she had been around Hayfield for an eternity. Once in passing, his mother mentioned that Mrs. Gloria babysat his grandmother once. Jeremiah just always assumed she had been around for at least ninety years.

When he went into Lipmann's, the woman attracted

him immediately. He guessed she was over six feet tall, but only by a hair. Her body was well built, though not overly muscular. She reminded him of an athlete; maybe a gymnast.

Her strawberry blonde hair almost glowed on top of her head. It wasn't just shiny; Jeremiah didn't care for shiny things. It reminded him of the painted saints with their halos glowing above their heads. It framed her tight and tan face, which was almost as golden as her hair. It was the face of a young, strong woman that was used to harsh realities. But all that paled in comparison to her eyes.

Her eyes were a crystal blue, any fairer they would have been translucent. When his misshapen eyes met hers, a warmth flowed through him. It was like a drink of warm milk, and he felt at so much peace that he momentarily forgot why he had stepped into the store in the first place. It wasn't their shocking color that made him pause. It was their slight imperfection.

Her blue-white eyes had rings around them. They were slight black rings that looked as if they were trying to reach each other to assault the blue. He was torn between staring into them and shielding away from them. It took all his energy to get to the back of the store for his groceries. Behind one of the aisles, he stopped and tried to calm himself. His heart was beating and his brow was flushed and sweaty.

*She could be the one.*

She was the perfect type. She seemed like she would fit his needs and his wants. Even though she looked healthy and strong, he was sure that he would have no problem with her. But something nagged at him.

He always sized women up this way. He would have his initial attraction, usually, because of some striking feature he couldn't help but become enamored with. It could be anything from an incredible height, fiery hair, he even met a girl from Los Angeles with cat's eyes, though he was sure they were just contacts.

They were all perfect for him. He always wondered if the women that didn't make the cut were ever aware of how close they came to being his next date. They never knew, they just kept living their life in ignorant bliss.

But, eventually, he would find something that he just couldn't get past. They would be too dirty, or they would have a small imperfection like a crooked tooth or a lazy eye. Jeremiah was picky. He knew his filthy ways would earn him a place in Hell while his angelic mother scolded him from her heavenly perch. He couldn't afford to be haphazard.

But this girl's one imperfection, the black circles around the irises, didn't bother him. She was perfect for his sixth date. Yet, there was a feeling in his stomach, and he couldn't get past it.

From his truck, he stared at her while she sat in her car. She was on the phone, shaking her head and yelling at it every minute or so. *Why are you so mad darling?* Whoever she was trying to get a hold of was getting her ire.

*No one can make you happy like I can.*

She threw the phone to her passenger seat, and then her little Toyota came to life. She backed out of the parking space and headed for the street. Jeremiah turned on his truck and followed behind, careful not to get too close.

# CHAPTER FOURTEEN

Rachel stepped out of the shower, her naked body breathing in the steam. The encounter with the strange man from yesterday was barely a drop in the pool of her memories. She didn't bother grabbing a towel, she didn't like the way they scratched, despite their false fluffy exterior. She had to keep her skin, her whole body really, in the best shape possible. It was her job.

It was just a few minutes after nine in the evening and she still hadn't eaten. She considered getting Chinese food from her normal take out, but her appetite had been declining recently. Instead, she grabbed her laptop and reclined on the couch. She placed the warm machine on her thighs so that she could check she had sent in her paper to her professor. It was Friday night, and she wanted to make sure that it was submitted before her weekend became too busy to do school work.

Relief flooded her, she was sure she would get a good grade on it. Mr. Holland was a good professor. Even though she had caught him looking at her for longer than he looked at others, he never made a pass at her. She respected him for that, especially since there was a picture of his wife and two children on his desk. Little facts like that didn't stop some of her professors.

It was one of her favorite classes, too. She was always good with money and numbers. When she graduated high school and got accepted to the University of Texas's Economics program, she dropped everything in Florida and moved to a little apartment just outside of the city.

Unfortunately, being good with money and understanding money hadn't made her any money. Her family was less than poor, and she was only so-so with grades. With no tuition assistance from her parents, and missing the cut-off for scholarships and grants, she had had to find another way to make money.

When she first arrived in Hayfield, she instantly fell in love with the quaint little town. It reminded her of her home in Florida, and the people were just as nice. They had the same southern charm, minus the beach tans. But, she managed to develop a new appreciation of farmer's tans.

She began working the week she moved there. It was a few months before classes started, and she wanted to make as much money as she could. In the morning, she worked at a local coffee shop serving all the commuters who drove into Dallas every morning. In the afternoon, she would change into her second uniform and drive the forty minutes across Hayfield, where she waitressed at a restaurant near the center of Fort Worth.

But when school started she had to cut one of the jobs. She gave up the coffee shop. She hated leaving, her coworkers were amazing and, on paper, the coffee shop paid more. But the tips she earned at the restaurant made up for the pay by almost double. Every morning, she attended classes and then she would change in the bathroom at school (or one of the teacher's offices) and then drive to Fort Worth and waitress all night.

Between classes, studying, and the job, she counted herself lucky when she could have at least four hours of sleep. She was just glad that she had left all her real friends in Florida. If they had been in Hayfield, she wouldn't have had time for them. Instead, her life was now barely more than a game of "how much sleep do you *really* need." She had almost finished her first semester when she got her first date offer.

Fridays' were the busiest. She had an extra class that day so she always went to school on Fridays in her waitress uniform. One particular Friday, the class had gotten out late so she had to speed to get to her job in time. Unfortunately, on her way into town, Fort Worth's finest pulled her over going fifteen above the speed limit.

The officer was cute, but she didn't try to flirt. She had learned in Florida that flirting didn't always work, so she just told him her story. She explained why she was speeding, and that she was sorry. Amazingly, he let her go with a smile and said he remembered those days in college and to be careful. It was the fastest traffic stop she had been in, but she was still late to work.

She rushed through the back of the restaurant to dodge her bosses. It was over thirty minutes past her start time, but when she went to clock in, she saw that her number was already active. It turned out that the ladies she worked with had covered for her.

She was the youngest waitress there, by at least five

years. They had all taken her under their wing when she started working. It was her age, coupled with the fact that she was so far away from home.

They would ask her about her grades and gave her advice when she was feeling down. She thanked her surrogate mothers and went straight to work. That brought her to the man that would change everything.

Mr. Armstrong had come in for a drink, but there had been no room at the bar. Instead, the hostess sat him in Rachel's section. She took his drink order: two fingers of Glenfiddich, neat. She still remembered it. She brought him his drink, and he sat there and sipped it in silence, watching the people in the restaurant.

In between tables, she had snuck to the back of the bar where she thought she was out of sight and laid her head against the wall. The exhaustion was pulling at her very soul and she couldn't fathom doing this for three and half more years.

After a few moments, she recovered her composure and pinched her cheeks to make them bright and rosy. She went back to the tables and checked on all her customers, winding between the busy Friday night dinner dates, careful to not interrupt the ones that were trying to be intimate.

When she finally arrived back at Mr. Armstrong, he had a slight frown on his lips.

"Excuse me, sir, is something the matter with your drink? Or would you like something to eat?" He was already on his second round, but it didn't look as if it had been touched.

"Are you ok, Miss?" he asked, instead of answering the question. His Brooklyn accent was a dead giveaway that he was not from Texas. Until then, she hadn't thought that men away on business may need more than just a drink.

"Yes, Sir, just tired." Briefly, she recounted her work and school schedule. It was a calculated story. She knew that if she told it right, with only the tiniest bit of sadness but backed by heavy determination, she usually found herself with a better tip.

He listened, nodding at the right times while staying respectfully silent. Then he reached into his pocket and gave her his business card.

"You know, if you aren't too tired, I could use some company tomorrow night."

At first, she had thought that she was being asked out. It was something she was used to, but she made it a habit to never date someone that met her at work. She thought it was rude and unprofessional. Politely, she declined and tried to hand him back his card. He stood up and laughed.

"No, no. You misunderstand. Miss, I am married and past the dating time in my life. I have a business party tomorrow and require someone by my side that will make a good impression. Think about it. I can make it well worth your time." Then Mr. Armstrong smiled a slick grin that she would always remember. That Saturday night, Mr. Armstrong was her first customer.

# CHAPTER FIFTEEN

She closed the laptop and got up to grab panties and a shirt. The room was chilly but she didn't feel like turning up the heat and then becoming sweaty. It was always like that; she was one or the other. It only took a one-degree change on the thermostat to send her to one of the two extremes. Tip-toeing down her hall, she was careful not to let her feet touch the frigid fake wood floors.

A wave of icy cold thrust itself into her skin and goosebumps developed down her body as she stepped into her room. She didn't remember leaving the window open. Sometimes she left it open during the day to enjoy the warm

Texas air, but she was sure she hadn't done that today.

She walked over to the open pane, her skin prickled with something more than just goosebumps. Instinctively, she grabbed her shoulders and stopped in her tracks. The wind was not *that* cold. A different feeling washed over her.

*What was that?*

Was it her imagination, or was it real? She swore she saw eyes in the dark where there were no eyes. She was naked in her own place, just like she always was, but she never felt exposed until now.

Then it happened. She could feel the darkness creep from the shadows and circle around her vision.

*No! Not now, Abby, I'm not in danger!*

But was she? She didn't know what was outside that window. Normally, nothing more than a large bush out there, that permanently leaned to one side from getting too much wind one fall when it was first planted. That was before she lived there. But the darkness in her eyes was telling her different. The same darkness that had saved her before. She shook her head.

"No, please! Not now, I don't need you right now."

She shook her head and she smacked the side of her face. The blood rushed to her cheek, and that calmed her nerves. She looked back at the window, and the only darkness was the night air. The black had left her vision, and she pushed the window pane down, closing out the dark chill. There was a small lock on the frame and she clicked it closed, pressing it in again, just in case.

She turned and went to her dresser, grabbing her favorite pair of green, faux silk panties. They weren't the best to wear during the day when the air was hot and sticky, but they felt amazing to sleep in. In the second drawer, she pulled out the pair of high-end sweatpants one of her dates had bought her.

His name was long forgotten, but she kept the pants. They fit her just right and she wished she could wear them outside the house. They made her feel sexy no matter what her mood was. She slipped on the panties and then pulled up the fuzzy pajama pants. As she turned around, she admired her butt in the mirror and rubbed the muscular curve. She worked hard to get that firmness, and she was happy with it.

She turned off the lights and went to watch television in the living room. It was getting late, but she deserved a little release. She entertained the thought of picking up one of her textbooks and studying a little. But after a drink first.

She left her room, shaking her butt again in the mirror, laughing playfully to herself.

Jeremiah laughed from inside the closet.

# CHAPTER SIXTEEN

The bent over bush scratched against the back of his neck as he slid the window open. He laughed at her carelessness. No one leaves their window open. He wondered if this was a sign. He pulled himself through it, stopping just inside the window listening for Rachel. He didn't want to be caught. He threw one leg over the sill and then climbed the rest of the way in, crouching on the hard floor under the window.

*I do not like her, Jerry.*

"But I *do*. She's so beautiful, Mother. She reminds me of you."

*There is something not right about her. Go home. Wash yourself of all those nasty thoughts, Jerry. You are going to give your mother a heart attack.*

"You are *dead* Mother; your heart doesn't care anymore."

*Stop! Why do you have to be so hurtful?*

"Stop it! She's coming."

Jeremiah ducked into the closet as Rachel came in. Her naked body was a thing only God could have created Himself. The golden, tight, soft skin begged for his touch; for his teeth. Her smile was just as radiant as it had been in the store, even her perfect body paled in comparison to it. Her firm breasts barely bounced when she walked in, and it took all his willpower to stay hidden. He wanted her right then and there.

He wiped his mouth when she leaned over the window sill to look outside. He cursed his carelessness, thinking that he had given himself away. If it bothered her, she didn't let on. Instead, he turned towards the dresser in the room.

Her stomach was smooth and flat; not muscular but visibly strong. The skin barely made a wrinkle when she bent down to put on her panties and her pajama pants. She danced a little in the mirror and he stifled a laugh. She was so proud of her body. He was proud of her body too.

*I had a body like that, once.*

"Mother, please," he murmured into his hand, he couldn't risk her catching him. He wasn't quite sure how he was going to take her out on their date. Seeing her naked in her room revealed how that her body was much stronger than he had first thought.

She left the room while Jeremiah tried to decide his next course of action from inside the closet. Peeking from behind the door frame, he could see her turn the corner to the left after she walked down the hallway. Barely breathing, he slipped out of her closet and tip-toed out of the room and down the hall.

# CHAPTER SEVENTEEN

Rachel grabbed a frosted glass from the cabinet and filled it from the fridge. She had made a pitcher of half sweet tea and half lemonade the night before, and the chilled liquid gave her goosebumps again, relaxing her. Not having to work traditional job gave her time to enjoy life again.

"This is how a college kid is supposed to live, not slaving away at a meaningless job," she said with a little laugh.

Had her parents heard her say that they would have probably lectured her. Her family valued hard work over handouts. She had come to terms with her new arrangement, she figured that if men were willing to give her their hard-earned money just for the pleasure of her company (platonic or not), then she was providing a service. Truthfully, that *was* work. She thought back to something her father used to always say when she was growing up and wondering what her adult years would bring her.

"What was it? 'Find a job you love and you'll never...' what was the rest?" she asked the vodka on the counter.

She considered the bottle with its shiny silver label with the Cyrillic lettering. She wasn't a liquor snob but she loved this brand more than any other. But as she asked her question, she noticed the silver shiny label reflected a dark shadow back at Rachel that was out of place. It wasn't her reflection. It was coming from over her shoulder.

She jerked, but there was nothing there. She laughed at her own jumpiness. No one was behind her, no one had snuck around her to go into her living room. Her kitchen and living room were almost one giant living space, slightly divided by a small bar counter jutting from the wall. And she reassured herself that they were both empty except for her.

This place felt right to her. She chose the small rental home because of the combined kitchen and living room. She could cook in the kitchen while watching chef reality shows. While she didn't consider herself a "foodie," she wished she could be.

"You need to get a grip, Rachel," she muttered.

She glanced at the vodka bottle one more time. The shadow was gone. She wanted it to be a trick of the light or her tired mind. She shook her head ever so slightly. That shadow had been around for years; it was just her looking out for Rachel.

"Rachel, it's time to turn this Palmer into a Daly."

Smiling, she added what was in the bottle to what was in the glass. Mixing the new drink with a spoon, she took a sip. The sweet sting kissed her lips, and her nerves relaxed.

She held the cool glass to her bare chest and spun around, her bare feet squeaking on the linoleum. As she sipped from her glass again, she watched the reality cooking show from her vantage point in the kitchen.

"Mmmm, Mr. Gordon. Say 'fuck' again." She giggled and took another drink. She loved that rough British accent, she liked the drama and his rough attitude.

Quickly she wiped up the small ring she had made on the counter. She didn't consider herself a "neat freak," but for some reason, she needed to clean the little things in her house. Sometimes, she got little bugs in her mind when things were out of place. That started after meeting her friend nine years ago.

It didn't happen often, but sometimes she went into fits of cleaning. She would be doing nothing or working on school assignments, and the urge would hit her. It started as a tickle in the back of her mind and it grew to a burn over her consciousness.

She would stop whatever she was doing, and then go deep clean the bathroom. Or, she would strip the floors and wax them. Once she was with a guy, not a professional date, just a regular hook up. The man was so slimy that her skin itched at the mere thought of him. She had been with him when she suddenly stopped, leaving him with his own *little* problem and ran to get the wood polish. The rest of the date was spent cleaning and polishing every inch of her cabinets.

She took another sip from her Daly and left the kitchen. As she stepped around the bar into the living room, something soft brushed her foot. She glanced out of the corner of her eye; at nothing. *Must have been a trick of the mind. Too much Daly.* She giggled.

"Whatever…" She threw her half-bare body onto the couch and threw her legs over the opposite armrest. Grabbing the little accent pillow that had fallen to the floor, she propped it under her side sit up halfway on the couch.

As the burning sweetness and acidic comfort traveled across her tongue and down the back of her throat, she heard a creak from behind her. It sounded just like a footstep in the kitchen.

Shifting a little, she glanced over to her empty kitchen. She craned her neck a little further; over-extending the rotation in her long neck to look further behind her current position. The back of the couch was clear. She laughed at her own jumpiness.

"You need to chill, Rachel."

She stayed over-extended looking over her shoulder, running chewed nails across the itchy skin around her tight midsection. She stopped and grabbed the edge of the couch and pulled herself a little further into the twist. A loud pop reverberated from her lower back.

"So much better."

She took another sip of her drink and smiled. When she turned back to the T.V. a man was standing in her way.

# CHAPTER EIGHTEEN

Jeremiah screamed and Rachel's drink shattered against his nose sending blood and shards of glass through his vision. He grabbed his bloody nose and bent over, his eyes tearing with alcohol. The broken cartilage felt bumpy under his fingers.

It took him a moment but he regained his vision. Rachel was gone. He scanned the room that stretched out in front of him. She was in the kitchen, holding a long silver kitchen knife.

"Get the hell out of my house!"

Jeremiah shook his head in a long slow sweeping arc. This wasn't right, his dates never fought back. The women he took went with whatever he wanted. To be honest, they did sometimes scream; sometimes they even cried. But they didn't fight back. It was new, and it was different. He didn't like it.

*Awe, Janet cannot stand up to a woman. What are you, a poof?*

"Leave me alone, Mother! I can handle this!" he screamed at Rachel.

Rachel stopped moving and screaming. She stared at Jeremiah, frozen. Her body seemed to flicker, like a movie on TV that hadn't played just right. It happened so fast he couldn't even say for sure that he had actually seen it.

"Get out of here, Jerry!" Rachel screamed.

He didn't have time to contemplate how she knew his name. Instinctively, he fell to the ground as the blade flew by his face. She reached into the cabinet and pulled out another knife. But it was smaller than the last. Holding it over her head, she ran at him.

Her animalistic scream was deafening and unreal. Jeremiah froze in fear for a moment before he regained his composure and grabbed Rachel's extra pillow. Just as the knife came down, hungry for his neck, he caught it with the pillow. He twisted, and the knife wrenched free from her grip, falling to the ground.

He had a brief feeling of accomplishment. But Jeremiah missed the other hand coming at him from the very edge of his peripheral vision. Rachel's small, but sharp, knuckles contacted his ear and a pop echoed through his skull.

The sounds of Rachel's house echoed around him. Shaking his head couldn't fix it. He could see her screaming, but it seemed so far away. She screamed louder.

"Get out!" Her command was distant, but Jeremiah could still feel the rage.

*Listen to her, Janet!* He wished that her voice had also gotten more distant, but it was as strong as ever.

"Both of you stop!" He shouted.

Rachel's face contorted as she tried to figure out who he was talking to. She stopped for only a breath of a second in confusion. It was a second too long.

Jeremiah balled his fist and swung it at Rachel's eye. His knuckles caught her temple. Swaying, she tried to hold onto the wall next to her. He wound up his other fist and let it fly, like a cannon catching her in the jaw furiously. He could not have her getting away. She wouldn't belittle him like that.

Gurgling, she fell to the floor. The blow had knocked

her out along with a tooth. Jeremiah was positive her jaw was broken. A trickle of blood had started to flow out of the edge of her mouth.

*You have done it this time.*

"Oh, no. No, this is not good," he cupped his ears with his palms.

Jeremiah looked around at the chaos they had made. The stabbed pillow, the slice in the wall, the knife buried to the handle in the plaster, not to mention the blood mixing with her drink on the floor.

*You made a mess, boy.*

"I know, Mother. I'm sorry."

*Get this cleaned up before you leave.*

She was right, if he didn't clean this up perfectly it may tell police who had taken her. This place had just witnessed everything and a good detective, *like the one on television,* would be able to find all the answers.

Jeremiah left Rachel in the crumpled mess on the floor and went to the kitchen. He kneeled in front of the sink. It was the normal place to hold all the household cleaners. He looked through her supplies, hoping for anything that could clean up any traces of him in the house. What he found shocked him.

Rachel had three unopened bottles of bleach and one nearly empty. There was a half-empty box of steel wool stuffed to one corner and a box of sponges on the other. He thought that maybe, not everything was all bad. That perhaps, he was starting to have a better string of luck.

"Perfect."

Humming, he pulled out an unopened bottle of bleach and a sponge. He cleaned his filth from Rachel's house while she laid blacked out on the living room floor.

# CHAPTER NINETEEN

Rachel fidgeted in the back seat of the shiny Jeep. Chase had taken her on an amazing first date. It was Saturday night when they went out to a small restaurant that she had never been too before. They served the most bazaar food that he had assured was very fancy. It must have been true, seeing as there had been no prices on the menu.

"Rachel, if you have to ask the price, you can't afford it." His slick smile and dimples made Rachel flush.

"But I would have been happy just getting a pizza, Chase."

"You are worth so much more than pizza." He reached out and touched her hand, giving it a slight squeeze. She could have kissed him right then and there.

His words were sweet, but she would have been content with getting a pizza. As an average sixteen-year-old, she appreciated that there were people who had more money than her family did. It wasn't something she held against them, she was just taught to enjoy what she had. She didn't need all the fancy things, not really.

Chase was different. At seventeen, he was well beyond rich. Well, that's what everyone else at school said. Rachel knew his money was from his parents. But still, he had his own credit card and got a brand new black Jeep last Christmas.

He was out of her league, Rachel knew that. But the years on the track team, sprinting and jumping hurdles, had developed her slender body into something that even the choosiest of boys couldn't ignore. And he had chosen her.

After dinner and the beautiful sunset, he took her to the movies. He even let her pick the sappy comedy she and her girlfriends had been dying to see. She knew that would make them even more jealous.

It was during the movie that things had started getting difficult. About thirty minutes in, after Chase realized that the movie wasn't going to be something he liked, he draped his muscular and warm arm around her shoulder. Her stomach became hot when it rested across her. He was rubbing her opposite shoulder when he stopped and let his hand fall. It hung there for a few minutes when he squeezed her breast.

She didn't know how to react. He must have taken her lack of reaction as a good sign and he did it again. Rachel smacked his hand away and ran out of the theater to the girls' bathroom.

She didn't know why she was shaking. Chase was gorgeous. Any of her friends would have pushed her into oncoming traffic for a mere chance of being felt up by him. She looked at her flushed cheeks in the mirror and laughed at her own childishness.

"You're sixteen, Rachel. This is so stupid."

A lady walked into the bathroom and went straight to a stall. Rachel hadn't noticed her. She too busy putting herself down.

"Laura says she already slept with two guys. And you can't even let a boy touch you. You're such a baby."

Her reflection sneered back at her. But briefly, the reflection jumped. It didn't move, it was more like a skip that happens on an old CD when you are walking around.

"No…"

Her blue eyes, the kind that reminded her of crystals, started to turn dark. She closed them and tried to shake the change away, but it didn't help. When her reflection changed, it always felt the same. Her brain would become stifled as if a large blanket was being pulled over it. She could still think and still understand what was going on around her, but there was a disconnect between what she knew and what she could do about it.

"No, no. Not now. I am not in trouble."

"Why would you be in trouble, girlie?"

Rachel jumped at the new voice. The lady that she had barely noticed coming into the bathroom stood at the sink beside her.

"Do you need help?" She lowered her gaze, "Is someone hurting you hun?"

The blanket over her mind lifted as she realized what the lady was talking about.

"No, no. Its… uh… the time… you know?" She tried to pass it off.

"Yeah, I got you, honey, do you need something for it?"

"No, no. I have a pad."

"What about an Oxy?" She winked and held up her handbag. Rachel gave it serious consideration but passed. She needed to keep a clear head. Besides, she wasn't having any cramps.

By the time Rachel got back, the movie was nearly over. She had missed something important and was totally lost. Grabbing Chase's hand, she led him out of the theater. She told herself that he paid his dues.

That's what brought them to an access road that ran parallel with the highway. It wasn't romantic, not in the least, but it was isolated. She wasn't sure if she was ready for this, but in the back of her mind, she felt like she owed him. He had even hinted as much.

His hand was on her thigh. Her heart was beating out of her chest and she could barely breathe. When he leaned in to kiss her, she didn't stop him. His lips were warm, they almost stung with sweetness.

His body pushed against hers as he continued to kiss her. After she learned that she was a good kisser last year, she was used to her kisses being seductive. He pushed her on her back as his hand moved from her thigh to between her legs.

Her heart skipped when he pressed his palm between her legs. It was fleeting. She wasn't sure if this was how it was supposed to feel. It was clumsy and not pleasing at all like he was groping for a light switch in the dark.

He moved to her ear. The tingle was unbearable and she had to fight the urge to laugh. He started to move further down. His lips found her neck, but nothing else.

She knew this was not how it should feel. There were no sparks, no fluttering. His hands were clumsily palming the outside of her panties, while his lips pressed into the nape of her neck and her collarbone. If he was trying to find a special spot, he was lost.

Then it got worse. His hands were getting too rough; his kisses too deep. She started to get angry but tried to keep it under control. It was her part of the bargain; he had spent so much money on their date and even sat through her movie.

*I owe him.*

*You don't owe him anything.*

The voice was barely there, but all over the air. She caught her reflection in the window behind him. The night sky was black with pinpricks of light sparkling down at her.

In the aura of one of the stars, she caught a glimpse of her blackness.

"No…"

She didn't need saving. This was supposed to be special; this was supposed to be the best thing in her life. If Chase had heard her vocal protest, he didn't pay any mind to it.

"Ow!" he had nipped her chest. He had made his way around her top.

"I'm sorry, babe. I'll make it better."

His fingers pushed the hem of her panties down. Two of his wriggly fingers pressed into her, pushing past her lips without any warning. There was no pleasure, only piercing pain.

*Let me. You don't need to feel this.*

The black eyes stared back at her from the reflection. She couldn't stand where she was or what she was doing. Nodding, she let the black blanket cloud her mind. Abby took control, blocking out the night for eternity.

# CHAPTER TWENTY

Jeremiah stood in his bathroom, pulling the last frosted sliver of glass from his bleeding cheek. He had been so preoccupied with cleaning the house he hadn't realized that he had gotten glass in his skin from Rachel's uncalled for attack.

"So unladylike," he pouted as he dropped the blood-tipped tweezers in the sink.

*I told you she was not the one.*

"She is, Mother. I know she is. She's so pretty." He soaked the washcloth under the hot water and wiped his face with it. The heat brought more blood to the surface and it trickled in little tributaries, meeting into a river on his chin and splashing in the porcelain sink.

*Cold water, honey. Cold water will help stop the bleeding.*

"Thank you, Mother." She was always looking out for him.

Flicking the cold water on, he waited for the faucet to purge the heat and replace it with a colder stream. The icy water stung his hands as he soaked his washcloth under it. He wiped his face again and the blood slowed a little.

Once the flow was nothing more than just little shiny streaks on his skin, he left the bathroom and walked down the hall to the living room. The portrait stared down at him; waiting for an explanation. He averted his eyes, twisting his hands.

"She's different, Mother," he whispered.

*They all are, yet they are all the same. I am the only woman you need in your life.*

"But," he breathed, trying to catch himself but it didn't work. A tear welled in his eye. "But you left me, Mother!" he blurted.

*I know honey. It was my time. God needed me.*

"I need you," he dropped to his knees. His heart bubbled over in his chest as his body tried to keep itself calm. It was a losing battle. Salty tears ran down his wounded cheeks, stinging them as they dripped on the floor.

*Now, now. None of that crying. Who cries?*

"Janet cries..." he sniffled, wiping his fingers under his eyes.

*And who is my strong little man?*

"Jerry is your strong little man," he sniffled, but the tears had stopped. He looked up at the round face in the portrait with a half-hearted smile.

*Good. Now go treat your date to the time of her life.*

# CHAPTER TWENTY-ONE

Rachel was feeling the best she had ever felt in her eighteen years. She had gotten her acceptance letter from Texas, she received her results from her finals giving her a GPA of 3.8, and she was going out with Taylor tonight to celebrate.

She stood in front of the bathroom sink as she finished putting on her lip gloss. She could never bring herself to wear lipstick, but the gloss gave her lips a little extra pinkness, and her kisses an extra pop.

She pinched her cheeks to push a little extra blush into them and took one last look at herself in the mirror. She was wearing a shiny blue dress, long enough to be classy but short enough to be fun.

"You look good Rachel." She winked at herself.

"Yes, you do!" She giggled at her own reflection and ran to grab her purse. Taylor was waiting outside.

*** 

There was nothing special about where Taylor took them on their date. When they sat down at Chili's, he picked what she was going to eat.

"Hey which burger do you want, Rachel?" He glanced at the menu in front of him.

"I wasn't really feeling a burger; I was thinking of getting the quesadilla." She didn't care either way, but she had learned to play a little difficult. It drove the boys crazy.

"Yeah, but I have a coupon for burgers. Buy one, get one half off. Choose a burger."

*A coupon?* She couldn't believe it. *Who brings a coupon on a date?* She dismissed the frugality in favor of his green eyes. She could have drowned in those green eyes.

When they had finished and he used his *coupon* to pay for dinner, they left. There was a crappy little drive-in theater at the edge of town. They played new movies, but on painfully small screens. No one from her school went there to watch movies, anyways.

He parked his car near the back of the open lot and

tuned the radio to the station that played the audio. The movie played, but she wasn't even paying attention. His lips were on hers, the steam filling the windows.

She loved this part. She never told any of her friends, but sometimes she liked kissing more than sex. The sex was for the guy, it made him feel good, gave him release. She never had a release from sex, not even her first time in the back of that Jeep. From what she could remember.

But kissing; kissing melted her. It was so much more sensual and pleasing than penetration could ever be. Unfortunately, Taylor wasn't a good kisser. There was too much gaping space between his lips, but he didn't use the space to put his tongue in her mouth.

Using her lips, she tried to coerce a better technique out of him. She might as well have been trying to get a slug to learn algebra. Hoping it would get better, she kept on. Until he went too far.

His hand left her shoulder and grabbed between her legs. No finesse, no sweetness, nothing to want her to keep him going. Besides, this was only their second date, they hadn't done more than make out occasionally. She didn't think that she had given him any inclination that she was going to put out. Especially not for a *coupon*.

She stifled laughter. He must have heard her because he stopped kissing her, pushing away.

"What was that?"

"Nothing, Taylor, just had a funny thought. No worries." She grabbed his collar, "come back here and kiss me."

There was a question on his lips, a statement in his eyes, but he kept both to himself. He leaned back in to kiss her, rushing his hands back on the inside of her thigh, hiking up her little blue dress.

*No.*

She felt her heart slow down and her mind fog. She knew. Abby was coming to her rescue. Rachel didn't need her. She could take care of herself.

"Stop."

"Stop what? You know you want this. Look at that dress you teased me with."

He pushed her back in the seat and climbed on top of her. Hot breath bathed her face as he fumbled with his zipper. *This asshole can't even find his dick.*

"No, Taylor. I said stop."

He ignored her. There was a light in his eyes as he found his zipper, the metal clink of his fly opening.

"Taylor stop. Now. I'm serious."

She put her hands on his chest and pushed, but he didn't move. At that moment, she became worried. She had always considered herself strong, self-reliant, able to take on anything. But he was stronger than her, heavier than her, she couldn't push him off. The black fog clouded her eyes. Abby was coming to her rescue. *Do I need you?*

Instinctively, Rachel shot her leg out placing her knee into his stomach. This gave him more access to her silken panties and Taylor took that as a good sign. But that wasn't Rachel's intention. That wasn't what Abby wanted to do either.

She thrust her knee into his side, the soft muscles moved for her knee cap and he fell back on his ass, clutching his body.

"You bitch. You are going to love this whether you want to or not."

"You will not touch her again."

Taylor lunged. His hands found her neck and squeezed. She could feel the pulse in his fingertips through her skin, just as she felt the pulse of his heart through his penis pressing against the outside of her panties.

"No, stop."

*Come on you little prick, you can't do anything with that baby pecker.*

He squeezed harder while his manhood threatened to penetrate her. Rachel stared into his green eyes. No longer calm and inviting, they were full of lust and rage. Suddenly, they were full of fear. He must have been looking back into hers.

Rachel felt the blanket wrap around her consciousness. Her hand flew up, catching her palm under his nose, making it crack like glass. Blood spurted from his nostrils and sprayed Rachel across the face.

The warm liquid heated her up. She wanted to feel more from the inside of his body.

He grasped his nose, trying to keep the blood from pooling on his seat.

"You fucking bitch, I'm going to kill you!"

The voice that came from deep within her body was not hers. She could hear it, she knew she was saying it, but she hadn't formed the words with her own mind.

"Not if I peel your skin off and eat it first!"

The words stopped him in his tracks. It was enough for Rachel. She pulled herself into a seated position and lunged at his face. Her fist came from behind her and contacted against his temple, causing his head to ricochet off the side of the door.

She grabbed his legs and pulled him towards her. She mounted him and continued to drive her fist into his face.

*You are a worthless man.*

His nose liquefied.

*You couldn't please a prostitute.*

His right eye exploded under her assault.

*How do you like being the bitch? How do you like it?*

Repeatedly, her knuckles dug into the soft pasty skin that hid his cruel face. The eye. The lips. The forehead. They fell, crumbled, became mush under her assault.

*This is fun!* She didn't know if the giggle was hers or Abby's. Right then, she didn't care.

His warm blood hugged her skin like a best friend. The slickness made her heart flutter. It was better than the best kiss she had ever had.

"Please... Stop... I'm sorry..."

His cries tickled her ears. A slick feeling filled her panties and she ground against him as she continued to slaughter his face. It was the best feeling Rachel had ever had.

*No, this is Abby.*

*No, Rachel, this is us.*

His face stopped resisting her punches. A white light erupted from between her legs and spread a fiery tingle throughout her entire body. She fell back against the opposite side of the back seat so she could bask in the euphoria.

It was her first time. It was her first time, and it was heavenly.

As she tried to regain her breath, she was faintly aware of Taylor struggling to breathe. The blood pooling in his mouth was hindering him.

He would live, which was a shame. She looked down, noticing his fly open for the first time. Jabbing it hard, she was rewarded with a burst under her force and she had an aftershock of pleasure.

Opening the door, she enjoyed the cool night air on her walk home.

# CHAPTER TWENTY-TWO

Jeremiah sat naked in the kitchen chair downstairs, his sweaty skin sticking to the worn painted wood. He wanted to sit while he watched the unconscious Rachel. He wasn't ready to wake her just yet. When he had brought her down here to his special place, she didn't even stir when he tied her to the cold steel table; not even when he snapped her jaw back into place. He was happy that he had only dislocated it. She had such a nice smile, despite her missing tooth.

Her breasts rose and fell with each breath, her nipples were standing at attention. All for him, he was sure of it. He drooled when he was tying her down, but something kept him from having her. He didn't like them to be out; unaware that he was there. He was a gentleman; he couldn't be so boorish.

She was wearing that simple sleep pants that she had on when he had picked her up for their date. He didn't even bother to cover up her naked top. There wasn't any point to it, the weather was still warm. Since she lived in such a remote neighborhood; he didn't feel it necessary to cover her up on the way to his car.

The syringe was ready for her. He prepared so much more than he would have normally done for any other lady. She was more special, she needed to be treated differently.

Beyond her fighting back - which was most unpleasant - she *felt* different. His feelings for her were also different. He liked her lips but did not wish to have them. His blood pulsed with waves of lust at her body, but he felt the need to leave her clothed. Despite all the temptation, he didn't touch her. He didn't like feeling confused.

He sat with his legs crossed, with the elevated foot bouncing in rhythm to the song his mother had taught him, while he tried to figure out what to do with her. A harmony filled his mind while he waited for Rachel to wake up on her own. When she stirred, he put on his best smile.

"What... where am I?" her words were slow and careful.

She tried looking around but her bindings didn't let her. The bright halogen lamp from the examining table was pointed directly into her eyes, blinding her. She could move her head to the side. She could just barely look at Jeremiah.

"You… it's you. Let me go!" She struggled against the bindings as her arms flexed; her small but tight muscles pressed against her skin. The binding stretched slightly. Jeremiah worried briefly that she would be strong enough to break free from the leather lashings. He relaxed when she gave in.

"Why are you doing this?" There was a slight pleading to her raspy question.

She tried to look around the room, but the light in her face and her position made that difficult.

"You are so breathtaking, Rachel," Jeremiah said.

His sweaty palms twisted in his lap as his flaccid penis retreated in fear.

*Janet.*

"I'm so happy you came out with me tonight, Rachel." He smiled, but to his dismay, she did not agree.

"Let me go, you filthy fucking prick!" She lashed out against her bindings again, veins straining against the skin on her neck. It was time for the syringe.

"Shhh, this won't hurt a bit." He stood up, grabbing the syringe off the desk.

When he stepped up next to her, the heat that was coming from her half-naked body warmed the front of his legs. Cooing, he reached down and stroked her hair.

He nearly fell back when she lunged against her bindings, her teeth gnashing at him, aimed for his groin. She missed, but he felt the air brush his hairs.

"Yes, later. Later you can do that."

He pressed the hollow silver tip of the needle into her arm, finding her vein. Pressing the plunger with a soft deftness, he injected her with his clear, special drug.

"What the hell are you giving me? Stop!" She twisted and flailed against the bindings, breaking the needle off in her arm. The little silver barb shined as it stuck out from her skin; the pulse in her arm pushed back out of the hollow tube, letting out a small bit of shiny crimson.

Then Jeremiah saw the flicker again.

Rachel had screamed when the needle broke off in her skin. But just as quick as came, it left. Her body stilled as she stopped thrashing against the bindings. Calmly, she looked up at him, her black-rimmed, translucent blue eyes became clouded over. The pain on her lips was gone, instead, they curled into a wiry smile. She let out a raspy whisper.

"That hurts so *nicely*."

Jeremiah took a step back, staring at the broken syringe in his hand. *How could this be?* He had heard that some women *enjoyed* pain, that they wanted the pain, but he had never met one. Could this be one of them? He looked at her lips as they curled into a smile that was pure fire and seduction.

"You're not right, Rachel," he threw the broken syringe on the table and grabbed his scalpel.

"Mmm, yes. That one, next." She giggled, arching her back against the restraints. A look of *anticipation* on her face.

Jeremiah hesitated, looking at the homemade scalpel in his hands. He wasn't sure this was going the way he wanted. For the first time, Jeremiah felt unsure about what he was doing.

*Do it, Jerry. Do it for Mother.*

"Yes, Mother."

Taking a deep breath, he stepped closer to Rachel; still grinding against her restraints. He stared down at her half naked body as her skin moved across her muscles. It was the same body that had made his blood rush to the wrong parts of his anatomy. Her filthy body had seduced him; it needed to be fixed so it could not hurt another man. He sliced the blade through the center of her nipple.

The liquid ruby trailed down her breast, as a thick scream spouted from her lips. Jeremiah dropped his scalpel as he backed away from her. The scream was wrong.

A bright flush appeared in her cheeks as her hips ground back against the table. Her eyes rolled back in her head; her throat gulped in long deep breaths of air. She *enjoyed* it.

"No!" He screamed down at her. Unable to handle it anymore, he ran up the stairs away from the confusing reactions.

# CHAPTER TWENTY-THREE

Jeremiah's knees hit the carpet. He held his hand up in the air, grasping for comfort from the portrait.

"Mother! What is this woman? I don't think I can finish." He covered his face, sobbing into his fingers.

*You stop crying right now, Janet!*

"My name… is Jeremiah… Mother!"

*No! Jeremiah is a strong man's name. You do not deserve that name. You are acting like Janet right now. Stop your crying.*

"But she is evil, Mother, she is *wrong*."

*All women are evil. Only your Mother was pure and good.*

"I know, Mother."

*You must finish this, Jerry. She deserves this. She needs this. I need this.*

He looked up to the portrait for guidance. This was for them both.

"She's filth," he said, more to reassure himself.

*Exactly. What do we do with filth?*

"Clean it up, Mother."

*Yes, dear, clean it up.*

# CHAPTER TWENTY-FOUR

Jeremiah smiled, watching the blood flowing freely from her nipple tracing little rivers down her full breast. She was smiling back up at him. Bound by the leather restraint, she beckoned him with a long slender finger.

"Come here, Jeremiah. Your mother will never know."

"What? How did you…?" Distracted, he looked up from the shears in his hand.

"I know many things about you, Jeremiah." She blew a kiss through the air. Blood flushed to the surface of his cheeks betraying his deeper lust. He shook his head, he needed to get rid of her temptations. He didn't like what she was doing to him. Using his shears, he swept down on her mouth, snipping off the tawdry lips. Jeremiah screamed and dropped his shears.

Through Rachel's bloody smile, there was a row of sharpened teeth. They gnashed out at him, clicking in the air. Smugly, she relaxed back down on the table; smiling at his reaction. The ragged shavings of skin left around her mouth flailed uselessly as she attempted to blow another kiss at him. Her eyes twinkled at a visibly shivering Jeremiah.

"You… You're evil!" Jeremiah screamed as he backed away.

"Oh, I'm so much more than that, Jerry," she slurred slightly through her nightmarish grin. She bit into the air at Jeremiah again.

"Come here baby, come to Momma!" She licked the blood from her teeth, causing her to raise her hips into the air, beckoning him.

"No!" He cupped his ears and ran past her into the Letting Room. Quiet and cool, sometimes he went there to calm down; surrounded by his memories. He locked himself in to escape her taunts. Holding onto the blinking shackles hanging down from the ceiling in the center of the room; their tinkling chimed out a lullaby in his mind as he tried to cope with what Rachel was.

"Mother, please help."

*Get back in there!*

"But, Mother, she's evil," he sobbed.

*Then you need to kill her. Cleanse the evil from her body. I told you women were the harlots of Satan!*

"Mother, I'm scared."

He dropped his hands. The long narrow eyes of the drain looked back at him; reminding him of his purpose. The deep maroon stain looked like red tears on the inanimate face. The face shifted in his mind; he could see her black eyes looking back up at him in the hazy reflection.

*Remember that you are my son. You are not scared. You will cleanse the evil that is deep within her soul. That evil is something you have seen before, now deal with it.*

He dropped to his knees, banging them against the stained concrete. The sharp, shooting pain gave him a spark of energy. He tried to cradle the drain cover, to hold the face of his long-departed Mother.

"I won't let you down, Mother. I *will* make you proud."

*You have done such good work. You have always made me proud, Jeremiah Adam Black.*

He winced at his middle name. As if she had slapped him with it, despite her kind words.

"Mother. I'll be strong for you." A tear fell and shattered against the drain.

# CHAPTER TWENTY-FIVE

As he picked himself up off the blood-stained concrete floor, he took a deep breath to calm his nerves.

"She's just another woman," he mumbled. He took a calm breath in, followed by a slow breath out. He couldn't let his nerves get the better of him.

"If she is just a woman, then I have nothing to be afraid of." He thought about what his mother said.

"But if she is more than that, if she is truly evil beyond the evil that I have seen in this world, then I must do God's work. I will make God proud, even better I will make Mother proud."

He grabbed the steel door handle that led back to the main room. He took a few more deep breaths to prepare

himself for her taunts. Her seductiveness made him feel…
*dirty.*

He kept repeating the same thing under his breath to force a rhythm in his mind. *Just a woman. Just a woman. Just a woman. Just a woman.* When he opened the door the shiny, empty steel table greeted him.

*She's gone!*

Jeremiah fell against the table, grabbing the tattered ends of the leather bindings that had once held his beloved. They were ragged, cut through, but with a little effort. Realizing what he had done, he scanned the empty table and then under it. It was nowhere to be found.

*The scalpel! You incompetent child!*

Vulnerability crept over Jeremiah. Rachel was free and armed. Using the littlest of movements, he turned his head. There wasn't anyone else in the room with him.

The shadows that surrounded the room which comforted him, reached out to him. He grabbed the examination light; shining it into the four corners. The harsh halogen cut back the blackness, showing him the four dating stations.

There were the chains connected to simple pulleys. He didn't use that one very often. but sometimes he liked the way his dates extended for his viewing pleasure. Sometimes he went too far, but that was the hazard of a fun date.

In the next corner were jars for preserving delicacies. They were all empty but he liked to have a good supply, just in case. There was one jar upstairs waiting for him from his last date.

In the third corner was a tattered and torn teddy bear from a failed experiment. The idea came from some movie where the teddy bear was alive, part girl, part stuffed animal. He never remembered how it was done but he had tried three dates ago. It didn't turn out too well. But, he just couldn't bring himself to get rid of it.

In the final corner was the antique galvanized wash tub that was his great-grandmother's. His grandfather, being well to do in the neighborhood, purchased one of the new washing machines. His grandmother; however, wanted to keep it "just in case."

The stringy mop was propped up next to it, along with a pyramid of empty bottles of bleach. He couldn't bring himself to throw them away. He always thought he should recycle them… one day. There was no Rachel. She wasn't down there with him.

*She has gone upstairs. Jeremiah, you cannot let her get away. She is more evil than you know.*

The light fell to the floor with a thud, he went up the stairs, taking each step two at a time. He grabbed at the handle but his fingers slipped from the cold silver metal. *She locked me down here!* He was trapped.

Breathlessly, he tugged on the doorknob, trying to get it to succumbed to his strength. His heartbeat pulsed through his veins like a marching drum. He tugged harder and then he heard a click from the other side of the door. It flew open in his face, knocking Jeremiah backward down the stairs.

For the briefest of moments, he felt weightless. As he fell, a red jagged smile appeared in the black haze that filled his eyes. *Her smile is so pretty, like when you drop a glass on the floor.* The darkness engulfed him as he fell into its grasp.

The world went fuzzy as his head struck the edge of a step. He bounced against each sharp step on the way down. On instinct, he attempted to tuck and roll, banging his knees and elbows. Mercifully, he stopped as he slammed against the wall on the first landing.

It took him a little while to unwind himself from the tangled mess. His head throbbed; his joints ached. Daggers shot through his back as he reached up and grabbed the handrail above him. Despite the objections from his body, he pulled himself into a standing position.

He stood there, waiting for the world to come into focus. All he could make out was the open doorway ahead of him at the top of the stairs. The black looked down at him as if a cycloptic eye judging him.

*Dark?*

He hadn't turned the lights off when he came downstairs. He always kept the living room lights on at least, because his mother was afraid of the dark.

Taking only one step at a time, he ascended the staircase. The pain in his back and legs subsided, allowing him to shuffle his way up to the door. Each step sent waves through his body, compounding the throbbing in his head. He could feel his heartbeat pulsating faster with each step.

He stepped into the darkened doorway, trying to adjust from the lit basement to the dark kitchen. Grasping with clumsy fingers, he managed to find the little nub sticking out of the wall. He moved the switch up and down, but the comforting light didn't appear.

"Mother..." he whined in the darkness. He knew she wouldn't be there; it was more instinct than a need. So, the answer that came back from the darkness sent a shiver down his spine.

"Yessssss," Rachel hissed. Jeremiah did not like that she was still in the house. *What kind of woman stays? Why wouldn't she run for help?* She may not be the one that needed help though.

The darkness didn't worry him too much. He had lived in this house his entire life, he knew this house better than anybody. His mother even said that he had been born in the house, upstairs in her childhood bedroom. His grandfather did not believe in doctors so Jeremiah came into this world in the comfort of these four walls.

He moved to his right, past the light switch, counting the top drawers under the cabinets. When he came to the fourth one he opened it, careful not to let it squeak. He didn't want Rachel to know where he was. He pulled out the black flashlight, old and sturdy, that he used for power outages. The batteries hadn't been replaced in some time, but he was sure that it worked. A harsh yellow beam of light flooded the floor in front of him.

He passed the beam around the tiny kitchen, illuminating the old coffee maker and the rack of dishes. The corners of the room were bare, he was alone. The hall that led to the living room was in front of him, the washroom was behind him. He didn't think that she would go there. There was nothing, minus the old washer and dryer that barely worked anymore. But when the darkness had answered him, the voice seemed to come out of the very air around his ears. He couldn't pinpoint its origin in the house.

Nervously, he turned to face the small closed door. Flashlight at his side he grabbed the shiny brass knob. He turned it, careful to keep it from making even the slightest bit of noise. Steadying himself, he snapped his hand back, pulling the door open. He flooded the room with his light. It was empty. He had to pause to get his heart back in his chest where it belonged.

He left the washroom doorway and turned back into the dark kitchen. Towards the doorway to the living room, his bare feet moved with aching silence on the cool linoleum floor. He was the predator, *not her.* He kept the beam from the flashlight down so as not to illuminate too far ahead of him.

At the threshold of the living room, he clicked off the flashlight. He held his breath; listening for any hint of Rachel in the next room. There was a heavy breathing as she rustled with something in the darkness. *Rachel.*

He clicked the flashlight back on and used his hand to cover half the beam. Peeking around the corner there was an even blacker shadow moving in a small heap on the floor. He pointed it towards the moving mass in the middle of the room. Rachel's naked back was towards him, her spine pressed against the skin as she was doubled over something on the floor.

He stepped out from the doorway, squaring himself behind her. If she noticed his light or that he was there, she didn't show any signs. The way her naked shoulders moved made it seem that she was wrestling with something large. Then he noticed the portrait missing from its resting place on the wall.

"Mother!" He yelled without thinking. Rachel's head jerked up, turning in spasms from side to side, like a hound searching for its prey. She turned to look back over her shoulder, her hair flying wildly. It fell across her eyes as she looked at the intruder. Even though the burnt blonde hair masked her face, the bright black eyes could be seen clearly in the light. They looked like polished onyx; the translucent blue had vanished completely.

Whatever she was hiding from him, she was apparently done with. She threw it towards Jeremiah. It landed in front of him, sliding the last few inches to a stop at his feet. He shone his light down at the mess and screamed.

"Mother!"

But his mother was no longer in the portrait. A tattered silhouette was all that was left. Rachel had ripped her out. His light reflected from the floor visible through the hole.

His body went into the smallest of convulsions since his mind didn't know whether to rage or cry. His shakes traveled through his arms and into the flashlight, creating dancing shadows around him. He raised the flashlight back to Rachel as she stood up with her back still towards him. She turned her gaze back in front of her.

Her still half-clothed body, shook with silent laughter. Her hands shot up to the side of her face, trying to hide it.

"You monster!" He yelled. Her once silent laughter flew from her mouth; bouncing off the walls and echoing through the shadows. She spun around and Jeremiah swore that she had broken her spine in the process. The thought didn't last long. When he saw her clearly he screamed again.

Blood had traveled down her stomach, tracing the line across her abs, pooling in her tiny navel. There were maroon specks on her soft sweatpants. The small line moved in and out in rhythm to her laughter.

He stared. Rachel was holding his mother's likeness in front of her. Her shiny red tongue was poking through a hole that had been torn through the painted mouth. She licked the tattered lips, letting out a thick hiss.

"Come give Mother a kiss, Jerry! Just like old times!"

Her cackling cut through his mind and his fingers dropped the flashlight in disgust and fear. His body shook as her laughing grew louder and threatened to bring down the whole house.

On the floor, the yellow beam illuminated Rachel's bare feet. Out of the shadows, the painted face of Meredith Black fell on them. Jeremiah ran away from her into the kitchen. There was blood on the canvas as it floated through the beam of light. In his escape, he hadn't seen the look on Rachel's face. Her eyes were full of love and pity, but her shredded lips were full of hunger. In the darkness behind him, Rachel followed her date in the black of the room.

# CHAPTER TWENTY-SIX

Jeremiah felt like a rat cornered in the sewer, waiting for the alligator to snack on his head. Goosebumps formed on his skin in the coolness of the house. He didn't know if his shivers were from the air, or from Rachel.

He held the knife level with his stomach, his bare behind pressed against the furthest cabinets of the kitchen. He was waiting for her. He didn't like this feeling. Was this how his dates felt?

*No more thoughts like that, Jerry. You are stronger than her. You will be fine.*

Jeremiah's breaths came in irregular patterns, out of sync with his shivering. His fingertips pulsed as they wrapped around the black plastic handle of the largest kitchen knife he could find in the dark. He kept whispering under his breath.

"She's just a woman. She's just a woman."

The stars shone brightly in the sky, casting the faintest of light into the kitchen. It was just enough to outline Rachel coming into the room, her steps mechanical and lifeless. The stars twinkled around her hair. She swayed on her feet, staring at him. In that pale light, he could just make out her face.

Her jagged lips hung uselessly over her sharpened teeth. The corners of her mouth managed to curl up in the sharpest of smiles. Her cheeks blushed as they pulled her tattered lips further apart. She cocked her head to the side, looking at the knife.

She began to speak, but the hissing that came from her was unintelligible. The anger seethed from her pores into the blackness and she cupped her hands in front of her mouth. The shrill screech reminded him of a victim that he hadn't numbed. There was a glint on her cheek from the starlight and he realized that she was crying.

Her body twisted in the air. She screamed with the pain that he had inflicted on all the women before her. He feared what she would do to him, but the screams caused his blood to rise and his anatomy to grow hard.

Her violent twisting and harsh screams threatened to break her entire body when she stopped just as fast as she had started. She dropped her hands to her side. Her full, pouty lips curled up into a smile.

"How...how..." Jeremiah was speechless. She had her lips back. His eyes darted to her breasts. They were undamaged.

"I learned that when I came to Rachel. I wish I could have saved Meredith with it. I didn't know my own abilities at the time." She opened her arms wide, her head tilted to one side and her golden hair over her shoulder.

"Now, come give me a hug. For old time's sake?" Her fingers motioned him closer.

"Stay back! Don't come closer, Satan!" He screamed, brandishing the knife from his hips. She looked down at it as if she had suddenly remembered it was there.

"Sweet, sweet boy. What do you think you are you going to do with that?"

Even though her lips had returned, the blood from where she had been cut before flaked off her chin as she spoke. They fell into the darkness like burgundy snow.

Jeremiah couldn't wrap his thoughts around what she

was and what she was going to do. A wave of vomit escaped from his chest.

He lunged forward, driving the knife into her side. The point hit bone: her bottom rib. He twisted the blade, pushing it deeper into her body. He continued to drive it in until his hand met her skin.

He let go, taking a step back then running back into the living room. He didn't stop long enough to find out if his actions were successful. A howl came from behind him and echoed throughout the house. There wasn't a trace of pain in the scream. Then she began to laugh. When she finally spoke, the very shadows around him seemed to reverberate her words.

"Jerry, what did you do? You are going to be so filthy!" She cackled.

He ran over the mutilated portrait, heading to the staircase near the front door. He thought about leaving, running into the street for help. However, he pushed the thought away, he couldn't leave the house. What if a cop found him? How would he explain his *victim* was turning on him? Instead, he ran up the stairs.

A sickened giggled escaped his lips as the irony sunk in. He had always found it peculiar when his dates ran up the stairs to get away from him. They would just be trapping themselves. It's not like any of them ever thought to jump from the second story window to get away. Instead, they would go into one of the bedrooms; hiding in one of the large closets. Occasionally they found the bathroom. That one he never understood.

As the thoughts flooded his mind he instinctively ran to the place he felt the safest: *Mother's room*. He only went there when he was feeling at his worst. He didn't enjoy disturbing the peace she had left with her dying breath. But sometimes he needed to bury his face in the hand-stitched quilt covering the talcum powder and lye smelling mattress. He would relive the memories of his childhood with her to find comfort.

He burst through the door and where it crashed into the wall and bounced back at him. He grabbed it, shut it, and locked it closed. Bracing the door with his back, he scanned the room. The only place to hide was the closet. He dove for the foe-lattice door, pushing past the matte black dresses and pantsuits, finding the back wall. He traced it to the corner and curled into it. He was just able to reach to the doors from the corner, shutting it.

The smell of mothballs and soap filled his nose as he

tried to take deep calming breaths. He shut his eyes attempting to shut out his entrapment. He strained his ears to hear any noises from the house around him. There was an ever-so-subtle creak on wooden slats outside. He knew those sounds, they were footsteps climbing the stairs.

With each agonizing creak, his heart rate stuttered. She was getting closer to him. His knees were pressed against his chest and he held onto them, trying to think of his Mother, trying to find peace and love. Her words came harsh in his mind.

*You did this.*

"No Mother, no. I was a good boy. I was trying to clean her."

He rocked back and forth in the corner, shielded by moldy decaying dress, hugging his knees. He wanted to feel safe, but the creaks had continued. They had climbed the stairs, coming to the bedroom door. He worried that Rachel already knew the exact hiding place.

He held his breath, waiting for her to find his precarious hiding spot. There was a click; the lock had been opened to the bedroom. The hinges cried in agony as the old wooden door opened with aching slowness. Jeremiah bit his knee to stop from crying out in fear. He had to remind himself to breathe even if it was only with small quiet breaths.

He waited in the eternity of blackness in the closet; listening for the creaks to come into the room and make their way to the closet door. But there was only dead silence, he could hear his heart beating inside his ears. He knew it, she had found him, but why hadn't she gotten him?

He strained to hear through the blackness for any sign that she was about to strike. The beating of his heart was getting louder; his breaths shallower. He closed his eyes to block out any distraction that could take away from hearing her next moves.

The air around him became still. He held his breath, hoping that the change would help him.

Rachel's face came out of the shadows behind him in the closet as he looked the other way. Her long slender fingers wrapped themselves in an icy grip around his neck. He took a few choking breaths before her tongue snaked from her mouth and ran up the side of his cheek. The warm saliva tickled his chilling skin as she flicked her tongue inside of his ear. Then Jeremiah's world went completely blank.

# CHAPTER TWENTY-SEVEN

Jeremiah had finished saying his prayers when his mother came into his room. She stood in the doorway, watching over him. It was a comfort, knowing she was there. In seven years, he had never known anyone stronger than her.

"Did you say your prayers, Jeremiah?"

"Yes, Mother." He climbed into his bed, kicking his feet under the covers and rested his head on his small pillow.

She walked in and sat on the edge of the bed. The mattress barely moved. Jeremiah thought that she was like an angel, and the world was her cloud that she floated on. She folded her hands in her lap.

"Did you brush your teeth?"

"Yes, Mother," he said with a toothy smile. Sometimes he forgot, he didn't mean to, but it happened. Tonight, he remembered; he was very pleased with himself.

"You are a good boy." She patted him on the head.

Jeremiah beamed up at her. She didn't hand out praise often, so he knew it was genuine. Standing, she pressed the edges of the comforter under his shoulders and kissed his forehead. He was ready for bed, but there was something on his mind.

"Mother?"

She stood up, but nodded, waiting for Jeremiah to finish his question.

"During Scripture reading, we read about Adam and Eve again."

"Yes, honey. It is important to know why we suffer. It is the original sin."

"Yes, Mother. But I was wondering, is that why my middle name is Adam? And if it is, why would you name me after a sinner?" He braced himself. He didn't often question his mother. Her word was second only to the Bible's, but he genuinely wanted to know.

She sat back down on the edge of the bed with the sweetest smile Jeremiah had seen in a long time. "Jeremiah,

Adam was not a sinner. Not really. He was pure, made in God's image. Just like you were." She reached over and patted the top of his head, and his cheeks turned red with embarrassment.

"But then Eve caused him to sin. She disobeyed the Lord, cursing herself, and the innocent Adam."

"But wasn't it the Devil disguised as a snake that tricked her?" Jeremiah was getting confused.

"No son, the Devil did not trick her. He tempted her, saying that the fruit would give her all the insights and knowledge of God. He also said that the rule against eating it was put forth by God to keep them down. So, it was Eve's jealousy and pride that made her disobey. And because she was a woman, she forced Adam to do the same. And what do we know about women?"

"No woman can be trusted except for Mother because I came from her." He recited the line dutifully. He had learned it some years ago and made sure to recite it correctly at least once a day.

"Exactly, so Adam was not a sinner. He was pure. He was innocent. He was a victim. And he should be remembered as such." She smiled and made to get up. Jeremiah still had one more question.

"If Adam was so good, why didn't you make my first name Adam and Jeremiah my middle name?" He liked his name. But he still wanted to know.

He always knew when she was about to get angry, it was like the very air around her seethed at whatever had brought on her ire. If he had the mind to watch her eyes, he may have seen the flicker. As it was, he didn't watch her eyes, just her clenched fists.

"Adam was pure. Adam was innocent. You could never deserve that kind of recognition, Jerry. As it stands, your second name is Adam, because you can only hope to be second to his pureness and innocence."

She stood frozen beside his bed. He worried that she would strike him like she usually did when she was angry. Instead, her shoulders dropped. She turned and pulled the door closed behind her. Jeremiah was left with his new knowledge and after he finished crying he fell asleep.

# CHAPTER TWENTY-EIGHT

He had no sense of time. It was a year as much as if it was a minute before his mind came back to him. When Jeremiah's eyes finally opened, they were burned by a flood of fluorescent white light. The excruciating shining ring hung above him like a halo. He turned his head; the cold steel table kissed his cheek.

"What?"

He pulled his hands, but they didn't move at his command. A quick glance revealed the tan strips of leather clasped around his wrist, tied to the shiny silver examination table with the remnants of Rachel's bindings. They used to be long enough to allow his dates to feel some freedom; allowing at least superficial movement. But because of

Rachel, they had been cut so short that he could barely move them off the table.

From his small point of view, he could see his table and desk. He turned his head the other way and saw the door leading to the Letting Room. He couldn't see what was above him or down by his feet from his tied down position. A cold laugh came from the shadows.

"Oh, little Jerry." A hand came from above his vision, her delicate fingers caressed his chin.

"What have you done, Jerry?" Her face came into view. She looked different. Her hair was pulled back and the air around her smelled like lye. Her skin looked soft and bright pink as if she had just taken a scalding shower.

"Let me go," he said.

"Oh, Jerry, I'll let you, just like you were going to let me go."

She bent down, letting her bare breast tickle the inside of his arm. She pressed her cold soft lips against his. Her searching tongue pushing his mouth open, sinking deep into him, wrapping around his tongue like a wet snake. Jeremiah felt a tingle down his spine that traveled into his pelvis. The feeling was short lived. She drew the scalpel under his bottom lip, cutting clean through. The tip of the scalpel scratched across the top his teeth but she stopped short of severing the lip completely from his face.

A white fire speared his brain, his body could not register where on his face it was coming from. His whole head was in agony.

"Now, now, Janet, don't lose your senses." She smiled and disappeared back into the shadows.

Jeremiah's mind tried to push away the pain. He had never felt anything like this. His Mother knew how to take care of him after his punishments. He feared pain more than anything. The burning subsided as the shock was beginning to numb the feeling. The warm red life spilled over his chin, cascading in thick spurts down his neck onto the table. He turned his head, she was rummaging through his desk.

"Fentanyl. The syringe. Please," he gasped, his throat vibrating against the cut in his lip.

Facing him, she leaned against the desk with her arms wrapped around her bare chest. Pouting, she looked at the bottles and grabbed the vial he kept his fentanyl in.

"Isn't this what you gave to your... what did you call them, dates? That's a little twisted, Jerry. But you did give this to them. You wanted to be a good boy, didn't you?" She held the vial between her thumb and middle finger.

"Yes, I never really hurt anyone…" each word ripped at his lip, "I wasn't going to hurt you. Please, Rachel."

Each syllable was excruciating, sending convulsion through his body. Against his own desire, his arms pushed against the restraints in a feeble attempt to will the chemicals into his body without her help.

Her smiled disappeared. "You think *Rachel* could do any of this? You don't know anything about women, do you?" She tossed the vial over her shoulder, where it smashed against the concrete wall. The tinkling of glass shards was like rain behind her. He whimpered.

"You look so pathetic. You weren't like this before. Why did you pick on women?" She came to his side and ran her finger down his bare chest. Her nails drew circles below his belly bottom and flicked across the inside of his thigh. His body reacted on its own despite his trembling fear.

"So dirty." The effect pleased her as she slashed down with her other hand. Jeremiah braced for cut between his legs, but it never came. Instead, the scalpel severed the ties that were holding him to the table. Trailing her breast over his stomach, she cut the one on the other side of him.

He was free. She backed away, her eyes daring him to move now that his restraints were gone. He looked around, the blood falling down his chest from his open lip reminded him that if she wanted to kill him, she could have.

He jumped off the table, clenching his jaw attempting to keep his lip from shaking. She didn't move to stop him. He ran up the steps.

He listened but Rachel wasn't following him. *No, she said she wasn't Rachel. What does that mean?* He had the faint hope that she was letting him free. *Maybe she wants me to live with the knowledge that she can deface me.* It was a terrible thought, but he knew it was better to be alive.

He ran over the portrait cutout again and darted to the front door. His feet slammed against the floor while his naked body shook with adrenaline. He flung open the front door, running out of his house. He didn't care who saw him.

Even if it was a cop, they would just take him to jail. The jail was far away from his house. The jail was safe, locked away from whatever Rachel was now. When he crossed the threshold of the door and headed into the front yard, he didn't see a cop. Instead, Rachel stood with her arms akimbo, the moonlight sparkling on the sweat on her shoulders.

Her head flung backward, her body shaking with a sick mixture of laughing and a screeching coming from her belly. She looked back at him and in a blink they were nose to nose. Something came out of the black night, slamming against the side of his temple. Black engulfed his vision.

# CHAPTER TWENTY-NINE

Jeremiah awoke with a problem. Normally, he would have immediately run downstairs. He was old enough to know that Santa Clause wasn't real, but at thirteen, he still enjoyed Christmas morning. He loved the eggnog, especially if he had peppermint candy canes to crush and sprinkle on top.

But this morning, there was a mess under the blankets. While he was asleep, he sinned without realizing it had happened. He sat on the edge of his bed, the sticky yellow stain talking to him from behind his back. He needed to tell his Mother, he always told her everything.

He brushed his teeth, changed his underwear, and dressed. The sounds of his Mother shuffling around downstairs reached his ears. She was no doubt making a Christmas breakfast of sausage and gravy over freshly baked biscuits.

As he headed downstairs the warm, starchy sweetness filled the air. When he turned the corner, the soft, white glow of the lit Christmas tree greeted him, towering over a small mound of brightly wrapped presents. His excitement overshadowed his fear of her reaction.

As he stood in the doorway, she came through the other side of the kitchen. Her apron was covered in flour and her hair was matted to the sides of her head. The kitchen must have been really hot while she cooked. She stopped short when she came in.

"Good morning, Jeremiah. Merry Christmas… What is wrong honey, you look upset?"

Jeremiah shuffled his feet, staring down at the floor. "Mother, I need to tell you something."

The concern in her voice was palpable. "Alright son, come to the kitchen and tell me." She turned and retreated to where she came from.

He shuffled into the kitchen behind her. His mother was already sitting at the partially set table for breakfast. There was a tray of butter out to soften on the table. A large bowl was in the middle of the table lined with a cloth, no doubt ready for the biscuits to come out of the oven. There was a warming plate with a pot full of Christmas apple cider, sweet cinnamon wrapping itself around the smell of the spicy apple. As the inhaled, he could almost taste the hint of clove.

She patted the chair next to hers, the worn wood waiting for him to come sit down and tell her. He did so, careful not to look in her eyes. His flushed cheeks and shaking hands were from terror.

He sat down but he kept his eyes on the little sticks of cinnamon floating around in circles in the pot of cider. They looked like ships circling for war. He wished he could climb into one of those spice boats and sail away.

"Mother, I have sinned," he said, waiting for her retribution.

"Tell me what you have done." Her voice became scratchy and monotone.

From the corner of his vision, she sat upright, eyes half closed, with the utmost proper posture. She only did that when she was thinking very hard about his punishment. He knew those eyes of hers would have been clouded over by now. It was her way of dealing with him.

"I… last night… I dreamt of sin and it appeared on my sheets."

A wail erupted from deep within her, she threw her head down on the table and cried into the crook of her arm. Jeremiah felt empty inside, he hated disappointing her. He reached out, touching her arm gingerly. She shrieked and jumped up, throwing the chair to the ground in the process.

"My son has made the ultimate sin!"

Despair and anger rang through her voice, her face flush and her eyes a jet black. Her breaths came in deep labored gulps.

She rushed passed Jeremiah, her slipper-clad feet pounding on the floor. The little boats in the cider capsized with her tremors. Jeremiah stood up to follow her. He didn't want her angry with him. He wished he could have taken it back; he wished beyond anything that he had not had such a terrible night.

When he stepped into the living room, she was hunched over the fireplace. Jeremiah wondered why she would be feeding logs to the flames when it wasn't even cold. It usually was only lit once a month to burn important papers. That's when Jeremiah realized the brightly wrapped present were no longer under the tree.

"Mother! Why?" He screamed, rushing towards her. He wasn't sure what he was going to do but he didn't understand why she would ruin Christmas because of an accidental sin.

She turned with a jerk. Her eyes were a swirl of blackened rage; her hair was turning dry in the heat from the growing flames, giving her the appearance of the Devil himself. Her voice matched her looks.

"Christmas is for our Savior. The pure child." She grabbed the fireplace poker and jabbed at the brightly colored flames as they licked up the boxes that had held his Christmas happiness. "You are no pure child anymore. You have sinned and are a filthy *man*. You do not *deserve* Christmas. Ever!"

With her last word, she stabbed at a partially intact box. The fire had crippled the outside enough that with the force it busted open. The new pair of wingtips he had been asking for all year so that he could be just like his grandfather were engulfed in flames.

# CHAPTER THIRTY

A pain was twisting itself into Jeremiah's shoulders. He was faintly aware that his arms were above his head, pressing against his ears. His body felt heavy, the tips of his toes barely touched the rough concrete below him.

The pain made him cry out as only one eye opened. The other one was swollen shut. Even so, he could still tell he was in the Letting Room, shackled from the ceiling over the drain.

"You can't do this." He said to the darkness. Footsteps echoed in the air before he felt a warm body against his back. Rachel pressed herself into him.

"Why not, Jerry? Didn't you do this? Five times, I believe." She placed a fingertip between his shoulder blades.

It trailed across his back, tracing a line under his arm. Her finger came back down over his chest as she stepped in front of him.

Through his one good eye, he could make out her accusatory smile. She held the torn piece of canvas that had been his mother's portrait. His lips were numb from their mutilation, making it hard for him to speak.

"Don't... hurt... her," he managed to say through the hole in his lip. He needed Mother.

She looked at the piece of canvas in her hand, her head cocked to the side. "Jerry, this is a painting. Your mother is dead. You do know that, don't you?"

Tears were running slowly down his face, but he didn't want to cry. He was stronger than that. The tears increased when their saltines burned the open wound under his lip.

"Mother... sorry."

"She can't hear you Jerry. No one can. Only I can hear you cry... Baby Boy." She held the crumpled canvas in her hand, using her fingers to caress his chin. Using her free hand, she wiped away the tears that were pooling there.

"Just... don't... my Mother." He said, trying to fight through the words.

She spat, letting go of his chin. "This is what I think about your mother, Jerry."

Through his half-swollen vision, she took her empty hand and pulled down her sweatpants, exposing herself. Stunned, he watched as she shook out the canvas, and wiped between her legs with a long, slow motion. The flush in her cheeks was evident and Jeremiah let out a sob.

Rachel laughed and pulled out the dirty canvas, balling it back up. Pouting, she reached out, using the canvas to wipe the tears away from his cheeks. Jeremiah nearly wretched all over her.

"Your mother hurt herself. Diabetes? She killed herself, Jerry. You know that. She left us both." Lowering her eyes, there was a twinge of sadness in her voice, catching Jeremiah off guard.

"What... do you... mean, Rachel? Did you... know... Mother?"

"Ha, poor boy," she laughed, dropping the canvas to the floor, "I told you, I'm not Rachel."

Both his eyes were swollen, one from her and one from tears. The clotting started to deaden the pain in his lips, if only slightly. He studied Rachel, half believing that this was a different girl. That, maybe, he had gotten the wrong person. She had to be Rachel, the only difference being that her eyes were black as coal. All he could do was shake his head.

"You can call me Abby, your mother did when I came to her."

Feebly, he pulled against the shackles that held his arms up over his head. He was starting to lose the feelings in his hands. He was sure they would be better if they could find the neck of whoever was in front of him.

"What are you talking about?" he screamed. The vibrations caused a searing pain in his mouth and he fought the blackout at the edge of his mind.

"Your mother was so beautiful." She lamented.

Rachel ignored him, instead, she walked behind him. He tried to turn to face her, but he couldn't move. The strength was slipping from his body, and his feet could not fully touch the floor.

"What are you doing?" he called out over his shoulder.

She ignored him again. "She didn't deserve you. Even your grandfather thought so."

She came back around, holding a small curved object in her hands. "So I took you. Well, *we* took you, I needed her body to move. But you were mine, all the same. I tried so hard, but you still turned out to be… this." She motioned at his hanging naked body with her empty hand.

"My Mother raised a good boy!" His cries echoed in the cavernous room; they clashed with Abby's growing laughter.

"No! I raised a terrible boy. I came to her when she became a woman, just like I did to Rachel. I wanted to show that I could raise a child. Finally. But *No*… you had to turn out like *this*. A disgrace. I should have let you die inside your real mother."

Tears flowed openly down Jeremiah's cheeks. "You're the Devil. God save me!" he cried.

"Ha! I am no Devil. I told you, *Janet*, I am Abby, Abyzou. I stole you from your mother. I was your new mother!"

"No!" He cried, closing his eyes from her.

"Stop your crying! Stop it now, Janet!"

"My name is Jeremiah," he yelled.

"Not anymore!" The curved object jumped through the air, severing his manhood from his body. He passed out again from the blinding pain.

# CHAPTER THIRTY-ONE

Mother held his head under scalding water, it felt like it was eating away at his skin. He was careful not to open his mouth and scream, or he may accidentally ingest the soap. Instead, he took his punishment in stride. He knew he deserved it, he had burnt Mother's dinner.

Normally, she did the cooking for the two of them, but this was her birthday. She told him it would be special if he cooked her breakfast in bed, and he was up for the challenge. He was sixteen, but she still did not let him use the stove. She was always afraid that he would hurt himself.

In the kitchen, he filled up a tall glass most of the way with milk, adding two large spoonfuls of sugar. Using the small cast-iron skillet, he managed to fry a slice of ham. He even added a little honey to the frying butter to make it extra sweet for her.

He should have stopped there. Mother required two things at every meal: sweet milk and biscuits. Everything else could be changed, the meat, the dessert, even the vegetables (if there were any). He had put the biscuits in the oven when he started cooking, but he had forgotten to take them out in time.

Burned beyond recognition, they looked like two dull hockey pucks, filling the house with smoke. He felt so moronic. Sometimes, if he punished himself first, she would leave him to wallow in the self-inflicted pain; satisfied with his punishment. While the oven was still hot, he opened the door. He placed his hand on the underside of the top lip and his fingers sizzled as they touched the hot metal interior. For good measure, he slammed the door closed on his knuckles.

He had made too much noise. She came downstairs to check on all the racket. He tried his best to explain what had happened, showing her his swollen, red hand. It wasn't good enough for her.

By sixteen, Jeremiah knew the signs all too well. She would become completely still and her eyes would dig into him. While he met the gaze, he would see a slight flicker in the air around her. There was even a flicker in her eyes.

The flicker happened every time she got angry. It was as if a switch was flipped somewhere, turning her into a different person. It signaled the onslaught of punishment. Years later, a young girl he was dating would explain it to him in the basement. She would tell him what that flicker was and he would deny it. But, for now, all he knew was that he needed to run.

He had only made it a few steps before a hand wrapped around the back of his collar, lifting his small frame into the air. Mother was never very strong, often needing him to open jars or move furniture. But when the flicker came, she was unnaturally powerful. It scared Jeremiah.

She dragged him backward up the stairs to the master bathroom, not giving him time to stand up, letting his legs drag in front of him. His butt banged against the wooden steps until bruised. When they got to the doorway of the bathroom, she flung him, clothes and all, into the tub. He tried to reach a seated position. She turned the hot water tap to full.

As the hot stream filled the tub, she grabbed a box of Borax. She opened the spout with her teeth and poured the dry white powder over his head. The mixture burned his eyes and the small paper cuts on his fingertips.

He knew if she saw him cry, she would wash his tears away. He fought back the tears, but the sting of the powder mixing with the soap across his delicate skin was too much and more tears fell from his eyes.

"Oh, Janet, you are such a mess." She slid her fingers through his hairline, grabbing a large patch. She pushed his head under water, held him there for a few seconds, then pulled him back up on the brink of passing out. He gasped for air.

"No, still crying? Tsk, tsk." She dunked him again before he could close his mouth, the soap and water burning his throat. She held him there for nearly a minute when she brought him back above the surface of the water.

"Why must you be such a terrible boy?" The frustration and pity on her face were thick.

"I'm sorry, Mother. I'll try harder." He sucked back tears while managing to catch his breath.

"There, there. I know. Now, who loves Mother?" She cooed, waiting for his answer.

"I do."

"Yes, you do." She grinned and hugged his soaking

Cloth-wrapped body to her dress. She whispered in his ear with all the love a mother could have for her child, "Now, clean up your mess.

# CHAPTER THIRTY-TWO

The smell of warm, slightly burning butter awakened Jeremiah. It was one of his favorite smells. His eyes fluttered opened, assaulted by the unexpected brightness.

The morning sun was peeking through the lone kitchen window, but the overhead light was still on. The bright white bulb cut into the long dark shadows caused by daybreak's light.

Head aching, he looked around. He couldn't remember coming down for breakfast this morning, but obviously, he had or he would not be here. He couldn't even remember going to bed. Even as an adult. he was not the best morning person.

Carefully, he turned his head. Even the slight

movement was terribly difficult. When his head finally finished the turn, there was a slender, feminine figure standing over the stove, dressed just like his Mother. His mind was clear enough to remember her, at least. But, unlike her, this woman had a slightly athletic frame.

Instead of dark brown hair, this lady was golden blonde; tied up in a bun on top of her head. She turned, her face showing only the tiniest bit of surprise that he was awake. A warm smile crawled across her lips.

"Good morning, Dear. Are you hungry?"

"I… I don't think…" He didn't know how to finish the sentence. His mind was still trying to wrap itself around who this person was in his kitchen. She looked like his Mother, there were the same opal swirls in her eyes, the same flicker in her smile. It *felt* like this was her, but something wasn't right.

*Mother passed away, didn't she?*

His head swam as he tried to remember the night before again. The effort made his brow hurt. He blinked slowly as he tried to focus. The only thing that his mind could grasp on to was her question.

*Am I hungry?*

He hadn't even thought about food, but then just as

he tried to dismiss the feeling of hunger, there was a dull ache in the bottom of his stomach. It radiated to his bowels, stabbing between his legs.

Could he be so hungry it hurt his legs? *Mother is always right.* He must have been hungry, he figured, she had said so.

"Yes... Mother."

She smiled, it was full of sweetness and love. Jeremiah was happy she wasn't dead like he had thought. He knew the voices were from her and not his imagination. Grabbing the gallon of milk from the fridge, she poured it into a glass from the cabinet.

She floated, step by step across the kitchen floor as she brought the glass to Jeremiah. She leaned in to kiss his forehead, then twirled to face the stove. The smell of lye and baby powder filled the air around him, stifling the smells of breakfast. It was familiar, it was home, it brought a calmness to his mind.

The sizzle of the hot butter in the cast iron skillet made him that much hungrier. Salivating, he watched as she dipped the pan, letting the cooked sausage link run into a dish she had sitting out on the counter. She called back over her shoulder.

"Salt and pepper, Honey?"

"Yes, Mother."

She seasoned his breakfast and brought it over to him. Kissing his temple, she sat the plate down. The spicy steam coming from the slightly charred meat, coupled with the crisp butter sauce made his mouth water. He licked his lips. There was something rough on the underside of them.

His hand moved to the crease above his chin. It was tender but rough under his fingertips. Delicate fibers where coming out of his chin, it felt like the laces on a football.

"Mother, what happened to my face?" He tried to remember anything before waking up in the kitchen for breakfast, but his head was still fuzzy. He couldn't think of any reason his face would be rough.

"Dear, you are a grown man. You need to shave once in a while."

He admired his Mother's kind wisdom. He hadn't thought that if he had woken up in the kitchen, he hadn't had time to shave that morning. It seemed to fit. Maybe he *did* need to shave. He made a mental note to do that after he finished breakfast.

He grabbed the knife and the fork, piercing the sausage, allowing a shining juice to spill onto the plate. He continued to slice down the center. She interrupted him.

"Small bites, Dear. Take small bites. It's better for your health."

She paused in the act of putting the milk back in the fridge, watching him with burning eyes. He laughed inside his own mind. It comforted him when she worried for no reason. Even now, he thought, she was worried about him finishing his breakfast correctly.

He moved the knife blade to the tip of the sausage so that he could slice a smaller bite. She must have overcooked the meat, it looked like the casing had split from the end giving the tip of the sausage a slight crown. He didn't mind, though. He would eat anything she gave him. She interjected again as he went to place the bite between his lips.

"Switch your fork to your right hand before taking a bite, we are not savages in this house."

He placed the knife down and switched the fork over. The sweet butter juice trickled down his tongue. His mother made great breakfast. He ate silently, enjoying the chewy meat and the foreign flavor. He wondered where she got this from. There was only one butcher in town and she refused to buy frozen sausages. He shrugged. He didn't care, he just knew that Mother only fed him the best.

# CHAPTER THIRTY-THREE

Leroy stood at the trunk of his old, government issued, Chevy Impala. He tried to rub the blood back into his face. This case was becoming more and more complicated.

He glanced at the tan line in his dark skin around his ring finger. The change in skin tone glowed in the flashing red and blue lights from his rear window. This case had taken its toll on everyone. Even his wife.

"Detective Banks, they found his wallet." The shaking voice cut through the dark night over the static from their radios.

He looked to see a young rookie hopping up to him. *With that goofy smile, he looks like a damn bunny hopping around the scene.* Leroy didn't know the young guy's name, but he couldn't have been out of the academy for more than a few months. Leroy wanted to be professional, but his silly grin was irritating him.

"Officer, this is a murder scene. Try not look so *happy*, alright?"

The young officer looked around as if, just at that very moment, he had become aware of all the cameras and flashing lights circled around them. The media was swarming around the scene like they always did. Flies around freshly dropped crap. The rookie hung his head.

"I'm sorry, Detective. But they found a wallet in his breast pocket. They wanted to wait for you before opening it."

Leroy walked past the boy, paused, and briefly tapped his shoulder. He tried to mumble something close to "thank you." He didn't linger any longer to say anything else.

In general, he didn't like the rookies. They always wanted someone to be their mentor, like little children looking for a parent to "show them the ropes." Little did any of the rookies know, some of the most senior guys on the force still didn't know what the "ropes" were. Any case could be a new challenge. Just as this case was taxing Leroy's skills.

A few years ago, the scene would have made him throw up every one of his dinners from the past week, but the Hayfield Serial Killer had been his case from the first victim. By now, he was becoming desensitized to the unique gruesomeness.

Instead, he was usually switching from tiredness to anger about the Feds trying to take the case away from him. Nothing but a bunch of suits trying to turn the case into a career maker. That wasn't to say that Leroy didn't need the help, though.

The first five victims had all been different. There was no obvious connection between any of them. They ran the gamut from a blonde-haired, blue-eyed, single college girl to a black, thirty-five-year-old doctor, mother of three. The one thing that had been the same was that they were all women. Except number six. Except for this one.

This was the killer's first male victim. Leroy thought that it was just a copycat murder. But the scene was too much like the others. He couldn't bring himself to believe that there could be *two* people in Hayfield that could do something like this.

The "John Doe" appeared to be in his late thirties or early forties. It was hard to tell if he had wrinkles because they still hadn't found all his face. The brow that was left did have sandy brown hairs. So, that was something.

The body was posed in a macabre position just like the five previous. This time, the body looked like an angel on top of a Christmas tree. *Well, not as Holy.* The arms were by the body's side, and the skin from the back had been pulled out; sprawled in a large sweeping shape. They looked just like wings—red and white wings.

The body even had a halo… of sorts. Leroy was sure that the "halo" was made up of what was missing from his vacant abdomen.

That was the final clue that that this was not a copycat. All the previous victims had been missing some type of body part. One girl had been missing her breast, one was missing her hip muscles, one was even missing both her eyes and liver.

His official response to media inquiries about the missing parts was that the killer was keeping them as trophies. However, Leroy had the gut feeling that he might be eating them. He didn't know why, but in his years as a detective he had a few "gut feelings" and they were usually correct.

This sixth victim was also missing parts. Besides his

face - which Leroy assumed wasn't taken just missing - the man had his genitals removed. The whole thing had been taken off, while the skin between his legs had been sewn back together. He looked like a doll, an angel doll.

Next to his body was a folded pile of clothes. It was as if the victim had undressed, folded his clothes neatly so that they wouldn't get wrinkled, and then laid down in the dirt to become what he was now.

Two of the crime scene technicians were crouched by the pile of clothes when he finally made it back to the site. They were holding large, yellow notepads jotting down… whatever they jotted down. Their exorbitant knowledge of science made his head hurt. He just knew that they were very smart and that he just needed to let them work. As he got closer one of the techs looked up at him. Her petite face was full of grim confusion.

"L.B., there isn't much here. It looks as if these clothes were washed recently. They smell like bleach. I'll know more when we get them back to the lab. It doesn't look good for much trace, though."

She took her Hayfield City Police hat off to wipe the sweat trickling down her temples. Her red-tented blonde ponytail was mated to her neck from the moisture in the evening air.

Leroy nodded. He liked that she called him "L.B." It meant that she knew him better than some people on the force. Those that didn't know him called him Detective Banks. He didn't like his last name. He preferred his first name Leroy or, better yet, L.B. Especially since that YouTube video came out from that game. For weeks, everyone started yelling his first name when he came into a room, mocking it.

"Thank you, Candice. One of the uniforms said you guys found a wallet?"

She handed him a clear evidence bag with a small worn leather wallet inside. He pulled it out and looked through the junk inside. Receipts, a good bit of cash, mostly in fives and ones, and a driver's license.

"Jeremiah Adam Black. Forty-five. From Hayfield." He read out loud.

Leroy pulled out his small notepad to write down the address on the driver's license. He signed his name on the bag's label and handed it back to Candice. When he got to his car, he pulled out his cellphone and called the office.

He told the dispatch where he was headed. He wanted

to see if the man had any relatives. There hadn't been any photos in the wallet, but there could still be someone at home waiting.

He drove away from the scene and the lights of the media. He didn't even need his GPS; he roughly knew of the neighborhood. The fourth victim had been found at the old Presbyterian church a few blocks away.

# CHAPTER THIRTY-FOUR

Jeremiah's home struck Leroy as a prop from a fifties sitcom. He half expected to see a man washing his wood-paneled station wagon out front, or a little old lady letting pies cool on the window sill. He hated that he was about to bring such a terrible cloud down on this happy little house.

Instead of parking in the driveway, he left his dusty silver car on the street. Their driveway was clear enough to hold another car, it only had an old beat up truck in it, but he wanted to keep a respectful distance.

The slightly off-white abode was accented by faded blue shutters and capped by a sun-bleached, blue shingled roof. The house didn't look run down. It just had the look of being well lived in. Judging by the age and the *feel* of the house, Leroy was certain that Mr. Black had lived here his entire life.

On his drive, he called in the man's information to see if he had any type of record or file with them. Dispatch couldn't find anything, no parking tickets, noise complaints, calls to the house. There was nothing. The man was like a ghost. Even the best people have the occasional parking ticket or speeding fine. It was as if he didn't exist.

Taking slow, respectful steps, he walked up the driveway. Instead of going straight to the front door, he walked towards the old truck, taking a quick glance through the windows. There didn't seem to be anything odd inside. In fact, there didn't seem to be anything at all inside. The upholstery was clean; the dashboard was shiny as if it had just been polished. He felt a little shameful that his car was so dirty. He slightly envied those people that could keep their vehicles looking like new.

At the front door, Leroy tried to see if there were any signs of a break-in. The door was intact. He couldn't see much inside because of the long curtain in each window. Knocking gently, he waited. There was a click on the other side of the door. He sidestepped, so he wasn't directly in front of the opening. Relief flooded him a warm pretty face poked itself out of the doorway, looking for her caller.

"Hello…?"

She turned her head to the left and jumped when she saw Leroy standing there.

Leroy pulled out his badge and held it up for her.

"Mrs. Black? Detective Leroy Banks, Hayfield Police. May I come inside and ask you a few questions?" He smiled, hoping his warm chocolate eyes would put her at ease.

She didn't seem to mind.

"Yes, of course. Come on in." She opened the door the rest of the way, then stepped away from it.

Leroy followed, taking in his surroundings quickly. He didn't like being locked inside someplace new. He wanted to see if there were signs that something was wrong or out of place.

He also liked to take a note of anything the person could hit him with. In the turmoil of utter grief, some people got violent. He had been assaulted by a widow or widower more than once before. Of course, he never faulted them for it, people can act a little crazy when their world is turned upside down.

There was a small dish of potpourri on the table that looked like it was porcelain. *That could hurt.* Everything else seemed normal… and clean. Everything looked *really* clean. The air was heavy with the smell of flowers, but not real ones. No, the smell was artificial, as if from one of those things that plug into a wall. There was a sting underneath the smell, like an artificial flower filled pool.

Mrs. Black walked him into the cozy living room and pointed at the floral couch against one wall. The upholstery was stale but soft. Mrs. Black sat on the opposite side of the small wooden coffee table. It separated him on the couch from her in the rocking chair. The chair looked as old as the house.

She crossed her legs and began to rock back and forth. She seemed unbelievably at ease for someone with a detective in their living room. Leroy made a mental note but decided he would revisit it later.

"What brings you here, Detective Banks?" She smiled and folded her hands in her lap.

"Ma'am, I'm sorry to inform you but we found the body of your husband tonight."

He braced himself. After the initial expected shock, there was a wide range of possible emotions. However, Mrs. Black didn't rage, she didn't cry, she didn't even blink.

This reaction was rare for Leroy, but he had seen it

before. The shock was so great that the spouse couldn't feel any emotion at all. It was as if their bodies went on autopilot and their minds checked out until they could find a better time to deal with what they had heard.

"What happened?" Her voice was calm and soft.

As a matter of policy, they didn't discuss facts with the family due to the integrity of the case. From a practical sense, though, he couldn't tell her because he didn't know exactly what happened either.

"We are still investigating, Mrs. Black. We have a few ideas. None that are strong enough to go on, just yet."

He sighed inwardly, he hated this part. He didn't know anyone he worked with that *enjoyed* telling people their loved ones were dead. But there were ones that could do it much better than he could. But it was his job to continue, for her sake at least.

Mrs. Black's face was etched in stone for the rest of his standard speech. He told her about the grief counselors that his department could offer. He gave her his business card; telling her that she was welcomed to call anytime she needed to talk. She must have been waiting for him to stop, because when he paused she tilted her head to the side and spoke.

"Can I get you something to drink? Tea? Coffee?" Her unblinking stare was disconcerting.

"I'm alright, Mrs. Black. Thank you." Leroy stood and walked towards the door. "Ma'am I have to be going. If you need anything, please don't hesitate to call." He smiled at her across the small living room.

When he turned to grabbed the doorknob, something painfully cold touched his arms. There were daggers of ice on his skin and he turned. Mrs. Black had closed the distance without a sound and grabbed his arm.

"Do you think you will find who did it?" Her eyes were searching in desperation.

*And fear.*

There was fear in her eyes. He thought that she must have been scared that whoever killed her husband would come after her. After all, he hadn't told her about the connection to the Hayfield Serial Killer.

"Ma'am, you have my word that I will do everything in my power to find the one responsible for your husband's death."

He placed his hand on hers, the one that was still holding him by the arm. Her skin was ice cold, but he could still feel the strength in those fingers. He pulled slightly, prying her hand off his arm. He needed to get back to work, even though he felt bad for her.

He left, and she caught the door behind him as he walked towards his car. There was a tickle on the back of his neck. Years of being on the streets had told him when there were eyes on him.

He turned to look back at the house. Mrs. Black was standing in the doorway, mostly hidden, as the door was only opened a few inches. But could see her clearly staring at him as he walked away.

Even in the dark, her gaze was as bright as day, not blinking. Fumbling for his keys, he looked over the top of his Chevy and saw that she was still standing in the door. A shiver snaked its way down his neck. There was something… *wrong*. He got in his car and drove back to the office.

# CHAPTER THIRTY-FIVE

Rachel watched the beautiful detective walk to his car. He was the epitome of "tall, dark, and handsome." His chocolate skin was smooth and tight. He got in his car and drove down the street. She wished he would have taken her up on the tea.

She closed the door and locked the deadbolt. He was such a gorgeous man, *Oh well.* She went to the kitchen and poured out the tea and coffee she had made in anticipation of the detective's visit. She couldn't drink it, anyway, she didn't feel like being asleep for half a day.

She knew he would eventually come to the house. She had carefully laid Jeremiah's clothes out with a purposefully sparse wallet that would lead the police to her door. She was expecting a cop, not a detective. She was pleasantly surprised.

She turned the light off in the kitchen after making sure the door to the basement was locked tight. She didn't want to go down there, anymore. Abby had taken over when she was with Jeremiah. It felt so good.

Abby (or Abyzou, as she had introduced herself to Rachel all those years ago) had saved her. She protected her from Jeremiah's pain. She had *fixed* the problem.

Normally, when Abby took over, Rachel couldn't remember anything. It was as if she was protecting her, not only from the situation but the memories. But not with Jeremiah.

Rachel remembered the pain, she remembered the retribution. Best of all, she remembered the breakfast. She giggled as she headed upstairs to the bedroom.

Rachel was there with Abby when she set Jeremiah up. It was Rachel that had the idea to make him into an angel, and Abby had taken the advice. They were working together for the first time in years. They were becoming partners.

Rachel undressed when she got to the bedroom. She folded her clothes, then stripped off her bra and draped it over her folded garments. She pulled down her panties and went to place them in her pile to wear again tomorrow. Instead, she threw them to the side with dirty clothes. She had gotten them filthy.

*Guess he was a little too tall, dark, and handsome.*

She smiled and went to the bathroom to get ready for bed. Looking at herself in the mirror, she could see the difference. She had always had the bluest of eyes, but recently the black of her pupils was starting to creep into her irises.

She walked back to the bed and laid down on top of the covers. It was warm in the house, so she figured she would be just fine without a blanket. Her butt tingled when she rolled over the sheets. She briefly thought about putting on panties just in case but she decided to not to bother. She was alone, and her nakedness was her only comfort now.

She stared at the wall. He hadn't been awake for the most of their time together, not really. Despite the little time they had, she and Jeremiah had connected. They had had good times together, whether he realized it or not. Now she felt safe and secure, knowing that the police hadn't connected her with the mutilation of her brief lover.

She rubbed her stomach in slow, small circles. The glow in her cheeks was unmistakable. It had only been a few nights, but a woman always knows. It's instinct. It's a knowledge that your body is changing even if it hasn't started to change outwardly.

She thought about names. She didn't like "Jeremiah Junior." She hated "juniors." She thought all babies should have their own identities. She made a mental note to look on the Internet for names in the morning.

She closed her eyes as her hand continued in small delicate circles over the warm feeling in her tummy. She didn't know if the heat was real or if it was in her mind. A warmth born of hope. The doctors had told her years ago that she would never know the miracle of having a baby growing inside her body. She, with the help of Abby, had proven them wrong. Jeremiah had left himself open to her.

Somewhere in the back of Rachel's mind, she must have known what Abby was, and that she wouldn't let Rachel enjoy the birth. But that was later, and right now Rachel was happy. She wanted to enjoy the feeling a little longer and hoped the nine months would fly by.

# CHAPTER ZERO
# MEREDITH'S ABBY

Meredith studied the blood on her sanitary napkin with disappointment. She was 18 this year and still, no child was within her. Papa had always said that a woman was a vessel, a bringer of babies, and if a woman could not bear children, then she was "as useless as a Jew in church."

Meredith never understood that phrase very well, there was a nice Jewish family at the end of the street and their daughter was always nice to her. She didn't even make fun of Meredith for not going to school; another useless endeavor for a woman, her parents had assured her.

She had never been with a man in a sinful way, but her mother had told her many times that a mere kiss was enough to transfer the filth of a man to a virgin young lady. She had found such a filthy man. Gabriel Russo was the most beautiful boy she had ever seen.

His black locks and golden skin made her stare open-mouthed the first time she saw him walking down the street. Her mother had seen her and had gotten upset.

"Don't go losing your head over some dago, Meredith. Your father would be furious." Her mother had warned her.

Meredith did lose her head though. A week ago, her mother needed butter from the market and, desperate to get out of the house, she nearly tore her gown jumping up to volunteer. Gabriel had gotten a job as a stock boy at the market.

Meredith waited until she was far enough down the street and out of sight from her parents. She pulled out the comb she had hidden within her brassiere and brushed her hair back over her ears, exposing her neck. She replaced it and pinched her cheeks, flushing them a blood rose color.

At the market, she slinked around the dry good aisle, attempting to look lost. It was only moments before Gabriel came up to her.

"Can I help you find something, ma'am?" He asked.

Meredith did her best to look seductive. She wasn't sure what that entailed, but she knew that her full figure was alluring to most men. She clutched her list in front of her. There was only one item on it but the move pressed her chest together, making it that much fuller.

"I am just having a problem finding the butter." She battered her eyes.

He motioned for her to follow him and he led her to the back of the store, where she knew the butter was.

"It's back here in the cooler section, miss." He grabbed a tub and handed it to her.

"Thank you so much. I guess I will check out then." She pouted as subtle as she could. The bait worked.

"You're Meredith, right?"

"Yes, how did you know?"

"My father goes to your father's bank." He leaned against the side of the cooler and his eyes wandered over her. She blushed and took a step closer.

"You should come over and say 'hi' then."

"Well, I just might have-" There was a yell from the end of the aisle.

"Get back to work you *batlen* I'm not paying you to mess around!" Mr. Lipmann, the store owner, yelled.

Meredith glanced at the interruption. That was when Gabriel had decided to steal a kiss on her cheek. She turned back to him just as his lips pressed against hers.

The heat in her face threatened to set her body on fire. His olive skin flushed and he darted into the back of the store before she could say anything. Meredith had a hard time checking out and walking back home without seeming too lightheaded. In her eighteen years, it had been her first kiss.

Meredith knew if that she had been allowed to go to school she could talk to him, and maybe even get another kiss. He was still going to school last fall, making him a little younger than she was. Her father wouldn't have it, especially now that her sin with that boy had brought on her visitor.

She shook the memories away and threw the pad in the wastebasket. She unwrapped another one, centering it in her panties and dressed back for dinner. Downstairs, she found her mother setting the table. She was murmuring to herself. She had always done that before but seemed to do it more after they found out about Sarah.

As Meredith helped her mother set the table, Sarah came in. Her rather large girth on her small frame made it hard for her to take steps in a straight line, but she managed to make her way to the table. She leaned against the chair and paused to catch her breath. Meredith seethed, she hated the fact that at her age she didn't have a child but her sister, four years her junior, was already eight months pregnant.

Sarah sat down at the table and Meredith scoffed. She didn't see why Sarah couldn't do her work while pregnant. She shouldn't have gotten herself knocked up if she couldn't handle it.

*I could handle it. I deserve that baby.*

There was a tingle down her spine and the world seemed to sway in front of her eyes. She grabbed the chair next to her and dropped the rolls. Her mother reached out and smacked her across the face.

"Those are your father's favorite. How could you?" She hissed and grabbed the rolls and tried to dust them off the best she could. She smiled at Meredith. "I won't tell your father." Meredith wasn't shocked, her mother often straddled the fence between fire and ice.

"I am sorry Mother; it must have been the curse." She shook her head and regained her composure. She never used to get the vapors this time of the month but she didn't know what else it could be. Her mother pretended not to hear her and went back to setting the table.

The dinner was eaten in silence. Her father was upset that Mr. Manson had been sentenced to life in jail. He always believed those Hollywood people were the icons of sin. He didn't necessarily think Mr. Manson was good for what he did, but he said he understood.

After dinner, Meredith went to her room. She changed into her night clothes and kneeled at the side of the bed, placing her elbows on the thin comforter and crossed her fingers.

"Dear Lord," She started, "Bless my family. Bless my mother and my father." Her eye started to twitch and she reached up to scratch it.

"And please bless my sister, despite her sin. Please do not let her slip from your graces in this terrible time in her…" Her hands fell apart and she had to grasp the bed for support. The room was spinning and there was a burn in her stomach. She grasped her sides as waves of sharp stabbing pains ripped through her abdomen.

"Momma!" She screamed out as she fell to her side and tears flowed from her eyes. Her mother, clad in her nightgown, burst through the door.

"What in the name of the Lord!" She swept down and cradled Meredith's head.

"Momma it hurts." The waves crashed against her stomach and she felt the sea spill warm between her legs.

"Shhh, Merry, shhh it'll pass. This is the curse that Eve earned us for her sin. It'll pass." She rocked Meredith back and forth.

Meredith knew the history. She also knew something was wrong and she didn't know what it was. She cried into her mother's sleeve. The pain finally subsided, or it got so great she couldn't feel it anymore, but eventually, she fell asleep. Her dreams were filled with death and sadness; she would never be with child.

*** 

Meredith woke the next morning in her bed, wrapped in her sheets. She faintly remembered her mom had tucked her in the night before. She dressed and headed downstairs. Her parents were sitting at the table; her father was sipping on his black coffee while her mother was cleaning the dishes from his breakfast.

"Good morning Father, good morning Mother." She greeted and sat down at the table across from her father, "I am sorry for being late to breakfast."

"It's okay Meredith, your mother told me what happened." He said through the steam coming from his cup.

Her mother touched his shoulder as she placed a subtle breakfast of toast and eggs in front of her. She started to take small bites, just like her mother had told her.

*Small bites equal a small waist.*

"Your sister needs to go to the hospital today to check on the… baby." He reserved the last word with a kind of disgust he normally held for the poor and hindered. Meredith continued to chew her eggs slowly. She knew where this conversation was going, she had to escort her sister to the hospital. She tried not to get excited. She loved to get out of the house and see different people.

Her father always left in the morning to go to the bank. Meredith was proud of her father's hard work, she knew they were well taken care of, but sometimes she wished her father would be home more. Her mother never left the house unless she went to the market to buy the groceries. It was left to Meredith to escort her harlot sister to the doctor's office.

"It's a shame that she is with child." Her father spoke almost matter-of-factly. Meredith stopped eating and held her breath. Her father hadn't spoken about her sister's unfortunate situation directly.

"You know you would be better suited as a mother." He commented, waiting for her to speak.

Her stomach started to cramp again and a haze came over her eyes. There was a small stab of pain in her mind as she imagined her sister's face.

*I'm not jealous, I would be a better mother.*

*Yes, you would. You should have had the child.*

Meredith shook her head. She wasn't sure where that had come from. She didn't talk to herself. That was the kind of thing a whack would do. Her mother sat beside her.

"Honey, please take care of your sister. She needs to see a better way." Her mother looked deep into her eyes and a new chill went through her spine and tingled her lower back. She nodded and continued to eat her eggs.

*Cleanse the sinner.*

\*\*\*

Meredith walked a few steps in front of Sarah. The sun was high above them, but the spring wind was nice and cool. The slight breeze made her breasts perk up. Her mother said she should stay humble and chaste, but she was proud of her body.

She always thought she was somewhat pretty. Her black curly hair swayed to the small of her back and her green eyes caused the boys to give her a second look at the market. Even some of the men looked at her. Her plump stomach and hips gave her a look of maturity beyond her age. She liked to be looked at. But her sister, she was the true draw.

Meredith had always been slightly jealous of Sarah. Since the age of twelve, she had the figure of a woman and looked nearly identical to their mother. Her chocolate hair was always soft and flowed like silk without even brushing it. Her brown eyes were piercing, not dull, matching her perfect, blemish-free skin. When Meredith had to deal with marks, she wanted to peel Sarah's skin off and wear it as her own.

*Now, now stay focused, child.*

Another alien thought in her mind. She shook her head and made sure Sarah was still behind her. Sarah was having difficulty walking up the sandy slope near the edge of the woods.

"Merry, are you sure this is the way to the hospital? I don't remember it being this hard to get there last month."

"You were not about to birth at any moment a month ago, Sarah." Meredith tried to say it with a smile, but her mind itched and her fingers tingled. Only a few more yards until they were far away from the city where Meredith and Sarah would be safe from prying eyes.

*This does not feel right. God, are You sure this is what You want to put in my heart?*

*They want you to do this, they told you to.*

Meredith didn't like the unthought-of thoughts. She wished she could ask her mother about them, she wondered if it was common to have them during a woman's time, but she didn't want to be taken away. Her father would have been most upset.

She concluded what she was going to do before they had left the house. Her sister was not worthy of the baby and her father had said so. She needed to please her father. She grabbed one of her mother's bread knives and wrapped it in an old kitchen rag. It hid nicely in her dress above her stomach, but below her breast. Her sister hadn't even noticed Meredith had it on her when they left the house.

Meredith stumbled over a small root that had reached up to grab her. Sarah gasped from behind her but made no move to help. Meredith found her footing and scoffed at her sister.

*I would never be that useless with a child.*

*I know dear.*

Meredith veered to the right, towards the edge of the woods.

"Merry, where are you going? Isn't the hospital that way?" She pointed over the side of the hill to their left. Sarah was correct, but she didn't know where they were going. Meredith continued to skirt the edge of the woods. A brilliant idea came to her.

"Sarah, what was that?" Meredith placed her hand to her ear and pretended to hear into the woods.

"I don't hear anything Merry." She mumbled, but her pace slowed and Meredith could see she was trying to hear what Meredith heard.

"It was just up here Sarah, I heard something. What if someone is in trouble?" Meredith pleaded. Before the baby, her sister had always been a bit of a bleeding heart but as the baby grew within her, Sarah had become selfish and self-centered.

"Merry, I'm tired." Sarah breathed heavily.

*Good, this will be easy for us.*

"Come on Sarah, you would want someone to help you," Meredith said.

She hid a wry smile and darted into the woods. She twisted through the trees until she found one that was rather large around the base.

*Here! Wait for her here!*

She ducked behind it, her knees burying deep in the undergrowth. She pulled the fabric of her dress from her breast and retrieved the bundle. Unwrapping the blade, it glinted in the light.

"Merry, where did you go?" Sarah cried out as she broke the tree line. Meredith ventured a peek. Sarah was taking gentle steps between the trees towards her. Unlike Meredith, Sarah always hated going into the woods and her current condition made her footsteps that more thunderous.

*She's almost near. Be ready.*

"Merry! Merry where did you go? I don't like this." Sarah walked past Meredith's tree but was looking in the opposite direction.

*Now!*

Meredith lunged towards Sarah, holding the knife overhead. A snapping twig brought Sarah's attention to Meredith. The knife found home in her collarbone, driving all the way through the shoulder. The sad look in Sarah's eyes would never leave Meredith. She had never hurt her sister.

*This is not pain; this is a cleanse!*

"Merry…why?" Sarah stepped back and fell to one knee. She looked up at Meredith and she almost seemed as if she was praying.

"I'm sorry, Merry." Sarah's eyes were wide with a glint of water on their edges.

*She is sorry, do I have to do this to her?*

*Do not get weak now!*

*But the pain?*

*Now!*

Meredith pulled the blade from Sarah's body and a red trail spurted from the wound and splashed across Meredith's face. Sarah continued to look up at her sister, her murderer. She cupped her stomach and Meredith sliced her sister across the neck. She would no longer feel pain.

Sarah fell backward, laying on the forest floor. The brown and gold leaves turned red and shiny as Sarah's eyes became dull and clouded. Meredith swore she heard a faint noise from Sarah's neck. She wondered if her sister had one last thing to say.

"No more talk from you, Sarah dear," Meredith said to the body as the Earth tried to take her in.

Straddling Sarah, Meredith bent over and ran a finger down the girl's cheek and kissed her forehead. She shuffled backwards and began her work.

It didn't take long to relieve the baby from his prison. Meredith had a steady hand as she carved up her sister. She whistled the little six-note tune her mother had taught her as a child.

She held the baby to her breast and soothed its small cry.

"You are so beautiful, baby." She hadn't thought of a name for her son yet. She didn't even know she was going to have a boy, secretly she had wanted a girl.

"You are so dirty, child." Meredith cooed. The mess on her hands and gown was thick and the baby was covered with a sticky mucus. She tried to wipe him down the best she could. She cut the cord and placed a hair clip on the end.

"Why are you crying, honey?" Meredith pulled down the top of her gown and moved one cup of her brassiere to expose her breast. The baby latched on and Meredith felt a warmth run through her body.

*Baby knows his mommy.*

The baby finished suckling and closed his eyes. As the baby slept, Meredith grabbed the knife and wiped it on Sarah's gown, her mother would be most upset if she returned it stained. She bundled it up with one hand, still holding the baby in the other arm, and tucked the knife back under her breast. She turned from her sister without so much as a look back.

Meredith made her way to the edge of the forest but stayed inside the tree line. Her gown was a mess. She just knew that if it got back to her father that she was walking around in such a disheveled way that he would be very disappointed.

She continued to wipe the baby, trying to rid him of the filth. She just seemed to spread it more over his small frame.

"You are so dirty; Father will be very unpleased."
*Such filth!*

There was a tightness in her chest, as she tried cleaning the baby while she walked. The need to clean him was insatiable. She wiped his face, harder and harder, with short frantic swipes.

The baby awoke under the assault and began to scream. His small little fist balled into the air and the skin that wasn't already red from the blood turned red from the cries.

"Hush honey, I will get you home soon enough."
Then a thought came to her. Another alien thought that

floated into her mind and dug itself into her consciousness. God had spoken to her directly because she was now a Mother.

"Hush my little Jeremiah. Mommy has you now."

See more from P. J. Mayhair at

**PJMayhair.com**

## Acknowledgements:

I am where I am today because of the love and support from the people around me and I want to thank them:

My mom, Joy. She instilled in me the love of reading and knowledge. She raised me to be the man I am today.

My wife and son, Maggie and Olli. They are my rock. They always believe in me.

My friends for allowing me to bounce ideas off them and asking them the most random questions. Caledonia, Amanda, John, and Kristy.

My fans. Readers and followers like you are why I do this. Thank you for joining me and reading.

A special thanks to Seth for helping rekindle my own fire and determination.

## About the Author:

P. J. Mayhair lives with his wife, son, and two dogs in Southern Maryland. He enjoys writing novels, short stories, and scripts. When he's not writing he's having bonfires, playing dinosaurs with his son, creating terrible drawings, and trying to find a way to create jellybean whiskey. You can follow him and his blog at pjmayhair.com.

www.ingramcontent.com/pod-product-compliance
Lightning Source LLC
Chambersburg PA
CBHW030922120626
46554CB00001B/237